William Linn Keese

William E. Burton, Actor, Author, and Manager

A Sketch of His Career with Recollections of His Perfomances

William Linn Keese

William E. Burton, Actor, Author, and Manager
A Sketch of His Career with Recollections of His Perfomances

ISBN/EAN: 9783337071462

Printed in Europe, USA, Canada, Australia, Japan

Cover: Foto ©Raphael Reischuk / pixelio.de

More available books at **www.hansebooks.com**

WILLIAM E. BURTON

WILLIAM E. BURTON

ACTOR, AUTHOR, AND MANAGER

A SKETCH OF HIS CAREER

WITH

RECOLLECTIONS OF HIS PERFORMANCES

BY

WILLIAM L. KEESE

ILLUSTRATED

NEW YORK & LONDON
G. P. PUTNAM'S SONS
The Knickerbocker Press
1885

TO

THE DAUGHTERS OF WILLIAM E. BURTON

PREFACE.

THE present volume was prompted by the thought that no adequate account of the late William E. Burton had been given to the public. During his life no man was better known, and his death called forth a universal expression of admiration for his genius and regret for his loss. In the many obituary notices by the press some brief details of his career were given ; but the narrative was necessarily confined to the narrow limits of a newspaper article. An actor so eminent—one of the greatest in his line the stage has known,— whose name is identified with certain delineations of character that died with him ; whose renown stamped his theatre with a celebrity distinct and remarkable; a Shakespearian scholar, whose devotion to the poet, attested

by the incomparable library he amassed, was
only equalled by his interpretation of the
master's spirit, surely is entitled to a more
pains-taking and a more extended record.   An
endeavor is here made to supply such need ;
and in the view taken of Burton as Actor,
Author, and Manager, the relation is from birth
to death.

In the preparation of this volume, the author
owns his indebtedness to Ireland's " Records
of the New York Stage," Wood's " Personal
Recollections," Wemyss's " Theatrical Biography," Hutton's " Plays and Players,"
Phelps's " Players of a Century," Clapp's
" Record of the Boston Stage," and Stone's
" Theatrical Reminiscences."   The writer also
gratefully acknowledges the assistance given
him by members of Mr. Burton's family, and
their loan to him of old play-bills, engravings,
letters, etc.   Mr. Matteson, of New York, may
also be mentioned in acknowledgment of
friendly aid.

The illustrations accompanying the memoir

will be viewed with interest. The frontispiece is from a daguerreotype, and has been chosen as a faithful likeness of the comedian. The *Bob Acres* is from a painting by T. Sully, Jr.; the *Dr. Ollapod* from a portrait by Henry Inman; the *Captain Cuttle* and *Aminadab Sleek* from daguerreotypes; the *Timothy Toodles* from a photograph. All the above were family possessions. The picture of the Chambers Street Theatre is from a water-color drawing in the collection of Thomas J. McKee, Esq.

Many shortcomings will doubtless be found in this book, and readers of it who are old play-goers may think of many things the author has missed. But we are told by Ruskin that there is "no purpose so great but that slight actions may help it," and by Wordsworth that

"Small service is true service while it lasts."

December, 1884.   W. L. K.

LIST OF ILLUSTRATIONS.

CONTENTS.

xi

WILLIAM E. BURTON.

1804–1860.

------

*"He was famous, sir, in his profession, and it was **his great
right to be so.**"*—SHAKESPEARE.

WILLIAM E. BURTON.

1804-1834.

WILLIAM EVANS BURTON, the son of William George Burton, an author of some repute, was born in London, September 24, 1804, and died in New York, February 10, 1860. His father was a printer, with a bent of mind toward theology, and gave expression to his views in a work entitled " Biblical Researches," published in the close of the last century. The son was classically educated in St. Paul's School in London, an institution where, before his day, Elliston and the elder Mathews were instructed ; and the father's design was to prepare him for the ministry. The parent's death, however, summoned him from his studies, and, at the age of eighteen, he assumed the direction of the printing-office, which he managed for the maintenance of his mother. It may be observed

3

that one of the specialties of the elder Burton's
business was the printing of classical works,
and the son's knowledge had often been of service in the matter of proof-reading. From the
printing-office he was led to the experiment of
editing a monthly magazine, thus early reveal-
ing an inclination toward the profession of letters which never wholly deserted him ; fostered
by sundry efforts of authorship in his native
land, and appearing subsequently, in this country, in his conduct of "The Gentleman's
Magazine" and "Literary Souvenir," and in
the compilation known as "Burton's Cyclo-
pædia of Wit and Humor."

The youthful experiment was not a substantial success, and did not long continue ; but his
editorship brought him into connection with
certain members of the dramatic profession,
and he was persuaded (we wonder if persuasion
were really needed !) to make a trial of his
stage ability by playing with a company of
amateurs. His success in this venture fore-
shadowed his destiny, and we find him in 1825

performing with a **provincial** company on the Norwich, Sussex, **and Kent circuits.**

We cannot help the indulgence, **at** this moment, **of a playful fancy** regarding Burton's **early efforts. Did he, in** the exemplification of tragedy, which he then aspired **to, reveal by** a single facial example the dawning **of a future** *Toodle?* **Could** imagination discover **in the** dagger **of** *Macbeth* the **hook, and in the** Thane himself the features, **of** *Ed'ard Cuttle, Mariner of England?* Did the thoughtful countenance **of** *Hamlet* suggest **in any** possible way **the** lugubriousness of an **incipient** *Sleek?* **Did he** make his Majesty George IV. laugh at Windsor, where, as tradition has it, he played before the king at this stage of his **career?** We know **not ;** but the **mask** of Melpomene had been thrown aside when, after another round of the provinces, with varying success, **but** gaining celebrity through **an** unusually wide range of parts, he made his first appearance in London in 1831, as *Wormwood,* in **" The** Lottery Ticket," a character **that became famous in**

his hands. This engagement was at the Pavil-
ion Theatre, and **was** a highly successful one.
The great Liston, just twice Burton's **age,** was
then at the Haymarket, and **we** can imagine
with what emulous admiration the young
comedian regarded the veteran actor. He
little dreamed that many of Liston's renowned
characters would **descend to him by** right **of**
ability and comic power! In the following
year (1832) Liston retired from the Haymarket,
"through a pique," as they **say, and** Burton
succeeded him ; but the audiences retained too
vivid a recollection of Liston's performances,
and the engagement was only moderately suc-
cessful. Recovering suddenly from **his** disaf-
fection, Liston returned **to the** Haymarket,
and Burton in his turn retired, to **once more**
make the rounds of the **provinces.** But he
bore with him one remembrance in connection
with the Haymarket that consoled him **for**
many a disappointment ; **and that** was the
thought of having played *Marall* to Edmund
Kean's *Sir Giles* **Overreach.** The story runs

that Mrs. **Glover,**[1] a leading actress of the company, objected for some reason to the *Marall,* **and** declared that **she or Burton** should be omitted in **the cast.** Kean, **despite** irregularities, still retained **a remnant** of his old sway, and he insisted **on** being supported **by** Burton. The result was that Mrs. Glover was compelled to yield, and in due **course** *Marall* appeared before a full **house,** containing many celebrities of the day. **It was at** this time, too, that a production **of** his **pen—the play of** " Ellen Wareham,"[2]—enjoyed **the** unusual distinction **of** being performed at **five London** theatres on the same evening. **A** year **and a** half went by in efforts to enhance his reputation, and it may be **said** that his career was **not free** from the vicissitudes that **frequently** attend dramatic

[1] Dr. Doran, in his " Annals of **the Stage,**" referring to Kean in various parts, **says :** " Among these, *Sir Giles* stands preeminent for its perfectness, from the first words, ' Still cloistered up,' to the last convulsive breath drawn by him in that famous *one* scene of the fifth act, in which, through his terrible intensity, he once made so experienced an **actress** as Mrs. Glover faint away,—not at all out of flattery, but from emotion."

[2] First produced, **May,** 1833.

itineracy. But through it all he gained ground
and advanced steadily in his profession. He
played almost every thing; his industry was
indefatigable, his will indomitable. The lamp
of experience never waned; and that knowledge gained from contact with the world and
human nature, was a preparation for events
and emergencies in another scene and another
land. For now his thoughts were turned
toward the United States, and in 1834 he determined to cross the ocean, and to take the
chance of fortune and of fame.

1834-1848.

Burton landed on our shores unheralded,
to begin the twenty-five years of the artistic
career which holds so conspicuous a place in
the annals of dramatic achievement. He was
not "brought over," and he came at his own
expense. He came, indeed, with the prestige
of having written "Ellen Wareham," and of
having made a comic character[1] famous by

---

[1] *Wormwood*, in "The Lottery Ticket."

fifty consecutive representations; but he was
simply announced as coming "from the Pá-
vilion Theatre, London," and he made his first
appearance in America at the Arch Street
Theatre, Philadelphia, under the management
of Maywood & Co., on September 3, 1824,
playing *Dr. Ollapod,* in Colman's " Poor Gentleman," and *Wormwood,* in "The Lottery Ticket."
Ollapod always remained one of Burton's most
effective parts. The portrait, on another page,
of the comedian in that character is from an
engraving by J. Sartain of a picture painted
from life by Henry Inman, in 1840.

There lies before us a bill (elsewhere reproduced) of the above theatre, dated Wednesday,
September 10, 1834, being the fourth night of
Burton's first engagement in this country.
The plays on the occasion were Sheridan's
comedy of "The Rivals" and the farce of
" The Lottery Ticket,"—which last seems to
have met with great favor, as the bill states it
to be a repetition, owing to "numerous enquiries having been made at the box-office";

thus beginning the **train of** similar " numerous
enquiries " with which, in the years to come,
his own box-office became familiar.   Burton
was the *Bob Acres* of the comedy and *Wormwood* in the farce.   Then at the age of thirty,
we can believe that the comedian's unfolding
genius gave full promise of the delightful
humor which clothed his *Acres* at **a** later day ;
and that in the *Wormwood* of the farce he
afforded glimpses **of** that wealth **of** comic
power which thereafter, and for so long, he
lavished for the amusement of **the** public.
Miss Pelham was the *Lydia Languish* and Miss
Elphinstone the *Julia*, English actresses of no
special distinction ; but it is interesting to note
that Miss **Elphinstone** became the second wife
of Sheridan **Knowles,** the author of a celebrated and far more popular *Julia* than the
lady **of "The** Rivals," and who appeared on
the Philadelphia stage of that year.

Something akin to his reception by the
audiences at **the** Haymarket in London, was
for a time Burton's experience in Philadelphia.

As the recollection of Liston by the London audience dwarfed the **efforts** of the youthful aspirant, so the memory **of Joseph** Jefferson, senior, (who played **in the city as late** as 1830,[1]) diluted the **interest felt in the** new **actor** by the Philadelphia **benches.**[2] But the native force **and humorous** capability **of the comedian were** destined **to** conquer indifference; and, although the creative genius which **informed his subsequent** delineations **was yet to** be made **clearly** manifest, **he soon** had **a secure** footing; **and a belief** was strengthening in the public mind **that an actor of** rare endowments and promise had ·**come** from the land of Munden, Elliston, **and Liston,** and one **who** might, **it was not too much to** say, worthily perpetuate the traditions of Jefferson.

On the fifth night of his engagement (September **12,** 1834) he played *Timothy Quaint,* **in** " The Soldier's Daughter," **and** *Tristam Sappy,* in the afterpiece **of** " Deaf **as a** Post," and so

---

[1] He died in 1832.

[2] So the memory of Burton in New York to-day may still be a warning of the danger of inviting comparison.

on through a round of characters in comedy
and farce—*Daffodil Twod*, among the latter, in
"The Ladies' Man "—written by himself—was
a great favorite. And it may here be said, in
passing, that the farce, which previous to Burton's advent had sunk into lethargy, revived
under his touch and became a vital point of
attraction. He made a great hit as *Guy Goodluck*, in " John Jones," in which part he sang a
comic song—" A Chapter of Accidents "—and
the fact leads us to remark that very few of
those who saw the comedian in his ripe prime
were aware of the musical talent he exhibited
in earlier years, and that he made a specialty
of introducing humorous ballads in his pieces,
and sang them with marked effect. A collection of such songs, entitled " Burton's Comic
Songster," was published in Philadelphia in
1850; and we were surprised, on looking it
over, at the quantity of mirthful verse he had
written and sung. The well-known ditty of
" The Cork Leg," it may be mentioned, was
written expressly for him.

ARCH STREET THEATRE.

FOURTH NIGHT of the Engagement of

Mr. BURTON,

On which occasion will be presented Sheridan's Comedy of

THE RIVALS.

BOB ACRES,	- - -	MR. BURTON
	LYDIA LANGUISH, Miss PELHAM.	
JULIA,	- - - - -	MISS ELPHINSTONE

Numerous enquiries having been made at the Box Office for a repetition of

THE LOTTERY TICKET,

It will be performed THIS EVENING.

WORMWOOD, - - - - MR. BURTON

WEDNESDAY EVENING, SEPTEMBER 10TH, 1834,

Will be presented the Comedy of

THE RIVALS;

OR,

A TRIP TO BATH.

Written by Richard Brinsley Sheridan, Esq.

BOB ACRES, - - - - - MR. BURTON

Sir Anthony Absolute,	Mr. Faulkner	Fag,	.	.	Mr. Crutar
Capt. Absolute,	Mr. Murdoch	Coachman,		.	Mr. Broad
Faulkland,	Mr. Wood	Cook's Boy,	.	.	Mr. Kelly
Sir Lucius O'Trigger,	Mr. Hamilton	Mrs. Malaprop,		.	Mrs. Jones
David,	Mr. Watson	Lucy,		.	Mrs. Thayer
Servant,	Mr. Eberle				

JULIA,	- - - -	MISS ELPHINSTONE
	LYDIA LANGUISH,	MISS PELHAM.

After which, the Laughable Farce of

THE LOTTERY TICKET.

WORMWOOD - - - - - MR. BURTON

Performed by him upwards of Fifty successive nights in London.

Capias,	Mr. Watson	Susan,	Mrs. Thayer
Charles,	Mr. Hamilton	Mrs. Corset,	Miss Armstrong

To-Morrow Evening, the Opera of

THE DEVIL'S BRIDGE.

COUNT BELLINO, - - - - - MR. HUNT

Being the Third Night of his Engagement.

The engagement of Burton with Maywood & Co. lasted two years, and was renewed for two more, during which period the comedian's powers greatly developed, and displayed remarkable versatility and dramatic resource. He widely extended his repertory, and was seen at the Arch and Chestnut Street theatres in a variety of comedy rôles and in innumerable farces. Among the many noted parts performed by him at various times we may name : *Ollapod*, in " The Poor Gentleman " ; *Doctor Pangloss*, in " The Heir at Law " ; *Farmer Ashfield*, in " Speed the Plough " ; *Goldfinch*, in " The Road to Ruin " ; *Billy Lackaday*, in " Sweethearts and Wives " ; *Tony Lumpkin*, in " She Stoops to Conquer " ; *Maw-worm*, in " The Hypocrite " ; *Sir Peter Teazle* and *Sir Oliver Surface*, in " The School for Scandal " ; *Mr. Dove* and *Mr. Coddle*, in " Married Life " ; *Dogberry* and *Verges*, in " Much Ado About Nothing " ; *Launcelot Gobbo*, in " The Merchant of Venice " ; *Bob Acres*, in " The Rivals " ;— the last-named character he played on one

occasion with the conjunction of the elder
Wallack as *Capt. Absolute*, Tyrone Power as
Sir Lucius O'Trigger, and Mr. Abbot (an actor
celebrated in his day) as *Falkland;* truly a
striking distribution. A few of the farces out
of the many were "The Lottery Ticket,"
"Sketches in India," "The Mummy" (so
famous in Chambers Street), "No Song No
Supper," "John Jones," "Deaf as a Post,"
"The Ladies' Man," and a piece called
"Cupid," which had won renown in England
through the acting of the famous John Reeve.

Burton's growing popularity was substan-
tially shown in the attendance at his regular
benefits. They were always bumpers, and oc-
casions of warm demonstrations of regard. He
was always ready, too, with his sympathy and
support where the claims of a professional
brother were in question. William B. Wood,
in his "Personal Recollections of the Stage,"
to which work we are indebted for much useful information, refers to an occurrence of the
kind as follows : "I must apologize for the

mention **here of a** circumstance purely personal, which proved **one** of the most gratifying **events** of my life. During the month of December, 1835, while acting in Chestnut Street, Burton called **me aside** between the acts, and with an expression **of** great pleasure, informed me that a **meeting for the** purpose of giving me a grand benefit **had** just adjourned, after completing **the** necessary arrangements. This was the first hint I ever had of this intention. The object was at once carried into effect, and **on the** 11th of January, 1836, **I** was honored by the presence of **one of** the most brilliant audiences ever assembled. * * * The following entertainment was offered : ' Three and Deuce,' two acts of ' Venice **Preserved,**' ' John of Paris,' ' Antony's Orations,' and **a** new song, and ' How to die for Love.' I was favored in these pieces with the valuable aid of Mr. Balls, **Mr.** J. Wallack, Mr. Abbot, Mrs. and Miss Watson, **Mr.** Wemyss, and Mr. Burton."

In the years while the comedian was advancing in his profession, and acquiring that knowledge of the stage which distinguished his subsequent management, his pen was not idle. He wrote several farces, and contributed stories and sketches to the periodicals of the day. These articles were widely read, and a collection of them was published by Peterson at a later date, with the title, "Waggeries and Vagaries"—a volume that has afforded entertainment to many readers of light literature. The literary taste referred to at the beginning of this narrative now sought indulgence, and in 1837 he started "The Gentleman's Magazine," a monthly publication of original miscellany. Articles of his own appeared in it from time to time, among others a graceful and appreciative sketch of his friend, James Wallack. He continued the editorship until July, 1839, when he associated Edgar A. Poe with him in the control.

To those who have paid any attention to the career of the gifted author of "The Raven," as depicted by various pens in recent years, it need scarcely be said that, though a man of genius, he was not without frailties ; and his warmest defenders will not deny that his life was marred by many irregularities of conduct. He was appointed editor of the magazine at a fixed salary, and the arrangement was such as to give him leisure to contribute to other **peri-odicals** and **to produce many** of his famous tales. " Happier now," says one of his biographers,[1] " than he had been for years past, for his prospects seemed assured, his work regular, interesting, and appreciated, his fame increasing, he writes to one friend **that he** ' has quite overcome the dangerous besetment,' and **to** another that he is ' a model of temperance and other virtues.' " For nearly a year he remained with Burton ; **" but,"** continues the same biographer, "so liable was he still to sudden relapses that the actor was never with confidence able to leave the **city.** Returning on one occasion after the regular day of publication, he found **the** number unfinished, and his editor incapable of duty. He left remonstrances to

[1] Henry Curwen, " Sorrow and Song." London, 1875.

the morrow, prepared the 'copy' himself, and
issued the magazine, and then to his astonish-
ment received a letter from his assistant, the
tone of which may be inferred from Burton's
answer : ' I am sorry you have thought it necessary to send me such a letter. Your troubles
have given a morbid tone to your feelings
which it is your duty to discourage. I myself
have been as severely handled by the world as
you can possibly have been, but my sufferings
have not tinged my mind with melancholy,
nor jaundiced my views of society. You must
rouse your energies, and if care assail you,
conquer it. I will gladly overlook the past. I
hope you will as easily fulfil your pledges for
the future. We shall agree very well, though
I cannot permit the magazine to be made a
vehicle for that sort of severity which you
think is so "successful with the mob." I am
truly much less anxious about making a monthly "sensation" than I am upon the point of
fairness. You must, my dear sir, get rid of
your avowed ill-feelings toward your brother

authors. You see I speak plainly; I cannot
do otherwise upon such a subject. You say
the people love havoc. I think they love justice. * * * But I wander from my design. I
accept your proposition to re-commence your
interrupted avocations upon the *Maga*. Let
us meet as if we had not exchanged letters.
Use more exercise, write when feelings prompt,
and be assured of my friendship. You will
soon regain a healthy activity of mind, and
laugh at your past vagaries.'" We think
nothing can be clearer than that Burton had
good cause for fault-finding, and that he was
more than considerate and just in his frank expression of feeling.

We do not intend to pursue the ill-starred
connection further. A more glaring offence
on Poe's part severed the relationship, and not
long thereafter the magazine was sold out to
Graham and merged in his " Casket," the consol-
idation ultimately to become "Graham's Magazine."

"The Literary Souvenir," an annual pub-

lished by Carey & Hart, was edited by Burton in
1838 and 1840, and its pages contained many of
his entertaining sketches.   He also contributed
to the " Knickerbocker Magazine " a series of
theatrical papers styled " The Actor's Alloquy."
Occasional starring tours belong to the chronicle of these years, and there lies before us a
bill of the American Theatre, Walnut Street,
dated October 14, 1839, announcing " First
night of the re-engagement of Mr. Burton,"
and also that " His Excellency Martin Van
Buren, President of the United States, will
honor the theatre with his presence."   The
President must have been greatly amused, for
not only did he see the comedian as *Tom Tape*
and *Peeping Tom*, but he also saw him " dance
with Mrs. Hunt the Minuet de la Cour and
Gavotte de Vestris."   Burton was fairly well
known now throughout the Union—except in
the town of Napoleon, on the Mississippi
River, where, if we may believe Mr. Davidge,
he found his Waterloo.   The engagement had
not been profitable, and his only hope was by

personally drumming for his benefit. So he
deposited a goodly number of tickets with the
bartender at the hotel where he was staying,
with a polite request that he would use his
best endeavor to get rid of them. The benefit
came off, and the attendance was very flatter-
ing. After the play the comedian invited several friends up to the bar, and there had the
satisfaction of learning that the man had managed to dispose of all the tickets entrusted to
him. This was very gratifying; but no offer
of settlement being made, he ventured to suggest that, as he was on the point of quitting
the town, he would like to have the pleasure
of receiving the insignificant amount of seventy-
ty-five cents for each piece of pasteboard deposited. Mr. Davidge says it takes a great
deal to astonish a barkeeper in Napoleon; but
this one was distanced. He surveyed Burton
for a quarter of a minute, and seeing not a
muscle move in the comedian's expressive
countenance, he said: " Look here, Mr. Billy
Burton, none of your infernal Northern tricks

here ; it won't do, no way! You told me to get rid of them tickets, and as I had promised I was bound to go straight through with it— *and by thunder, I was obliged to stand drinks to every man to take one !* " An audience may be uncultured if not lukewarm ; and the unimpressible community of Napoleon reminds us that the "Antigone" of Sophocles was once produced under Burton's management, and, on loud and repeated calls for the *author*, the comedian presented himself before the footlights and said: "Ladies and gentlemen, it would give me the greatest pleasure to introduce the author of the play ; but, unfortunately, he has been dead for more than twenty centuries, and I shall have to throw myself upon your indulgence."

Burton made his first appearance in New York October 31, 1837, at the old National Theatre in Leonard Street—then under the management of the elder Wallack—for the benefit of Samuel Woodworth, the poet, playing *Guy Goodluck*, in "John Jones"; and his

first appearance as a star was made at the same
theatre February 4, 1839, when **he** played *Billy
Lackaday*, in "Sweethearts and Wives," **and**
Guy Goodluck. **A** complimentary benefit was
given to **Mr.** Wallack in the same year, when
Burton played *Sir Simon Slack*, in "Spring **and**
Autumn." **The** opera of "Amilie ; or, The Love
Test" was produced **on the same** occasion. If
we mistake not, he was connected with the
management when the theatre was destroyed
by fire not long **after. He** also appeared at
Niblo's Garden as **a star in** this year, opening
June 25th, and was seen in a round **of** parts,
including **Gregory** *Thimblewell, Euclid Facile,
Ignatius Polyglott,* **and** *Tobias Munns*, in his
own farce **of "Forty** Winks." **He** first appeared on the Park stage June 2, **1840,** playing
Sir Timothy Stilton, **in** "Patrician **and** Parvenu," the occasion being **a** complimentary
benefit **to Peter** Richings; and **in** the same
month acted at Niblo's Garden. **At** his benefit
(July 6th) **he** played *Brown*, in "**Kill** and
Cure," and *Fluid* in "The Water Party." The

participation of the Cushman sisters in this
entertainment greatly enhanced its interest
and attractiveness.   In this year he fitted up
Cooke's circus-building in Chestnut Street,
Philadelphia, calling it the National Theatre.
He gathered a fine company and was very
prosperous.   Charlotte and Susan Cushman
appeared there, and the sterling comedians
Henry and Thomas Placide were among the
force.   The fairy piece, "The Naiad Queen,"
was there presented for the first time in the
United States, and brought wealth to the manager's coffers.   A large amount of his earnings
by this enterprise he invested in Nick Biddle's
United States Bank, and in the downfall of
that institution suffered severely.

In 1841, after a brief engagement at the
Providence theatre, he returned to New York,
and leased the rebuilt theatre corner of Leonard and Church streets, where his first appearance in New York had been made ; brought on
his Philadelphia company, and there established himself.   This was April 13, 1841, and

MR. BURTON AS DR. OLLARD

his first essay as manager in New York. He
transported all the beautiful scenery of " The
Naiad Queen," and reproduced the piece with
gratifying success. But a dread fatality seemed
to attend this temple of the drama. As, while
under Wallack's management, it was destroyed
by fire, so the same doom befell it under
Burton. In the height of prosperity the building was again consumed, and with it the elaborate and splendid scenery of "The Naiad
Queen." Of this calamity, F. C. Wemyss, in
his " Theatrical Biography," remarks : " On
this occasion a magnificent and extensive
wardrobe, the property of Mr. Burton, was
consumed, together with his private wardrobe,
manuscripts, books, and other articles of con-
siderable value. He was not insured to the
amount of a dollar. The citizens of New York
expressed their sympathy with the manager ;
and a complimentary benefit at the Park placed
a handsome sum at his disposal." Undaunted
by a disaster which would have utterly dis-
couraged most men, Burton again sought Phil-

adelphia, and **after** starring for a brief season
leased the Chestnut Street Theatre for **a** fresh
essay. There for a while he continued with
good fortune, until better prospects invited
him to Arch Street, where at last he located
with a view to permanency. Meeting now
with rich success, he determined to extend his
sphere of operation, and added in turn to his
lesseeship the Front Street Theatre, Baltimore,
and the theatre in Washington; so that in
1845–6 he was guiding the destinies of three
dramatic houses, distinguished for well-chosen
companies and **for** the admirable manner in
which the plays were mounted and cast. But
again the fiat of destiny was written in words of
flame. The Washington theatre, for the first
time in many years, was handsomely rewarding
its manager, when one night, during the performance, the scenery caught fire, and the
building was burnt to the ground. The Baltimore theatre was continued; but the lion's
share **of** attention **was** given to Arch Street,
and there for several years Burton enjoyed **a**

flow of prosperity; his fame increasing in public estimation; surprising and delighting all by his wonderful acting, **and** by the knowledge, taste, and liberality, **with** which he catered for his patrons. But New York was in the manager's thoughts **and** seemed **to** beckon him Northward. Perhaps Burton's prophetic gaze discerned **in the** great city **a** field **that** would **respond to** careful tillage, **and that the** rapid growth of the metropolis could not fail to give momentum **to** enterprise. Whatever the motive spring, **the step** was taken, and **in** 1848 the building known **as** Palmo's Opera-House became Burton's Theatre.

In this brief survey **of fourteen** years, the absence of detail in many instances **will be pardoned**, we hope, on a reflection of what it may suggest. We are aware of the interest attaching **to** strength **of** companies, citations of casts, and notes of special performance; and in all theatrical histories such details should evoke the most careful consideration. The Philadelphia record, however, is not always full and

clear on those points, as respects individual
careers, even in one so active and fruitful as
our subject's; for, so far as we know, there is
no history of the stage of that city which pre-
tends to do for its dramatic life what Ireland
has done for the New York stage—regarding which monument of painstaking fidelity,
William Winter, in the preface to his recent
admirable volume on "The Jeffersons," truly
says: "Every writer who touches upon the
history of the drama in America must ac-
knowledge his obligation for guidance and
aid to the thorough, faithful and suggestive
records made by the veteran historian, Joseph
N. Ireland." Yet, in depicting the career of
a great actor, many things are rendered subor-
dinate which in a history of the drama of any
given period would receive due prominence.
That the career of Burton in Philadelphia from
1834 to 1848 embraced much of its stage history during those years, will, of course, be un-
derstood; and we shall be sorry if our readers,
at the same time, fail to discern the industry,

sagacity, courage, and varied powers—with which the actor, author, and manager, illustrated those years—suggested by this recital.

We now approach a period within the memory of many persons now living. Some few octogenarians may survive who can recall Burton's performances of over forty years ago ; but they must be **few** indeed ; and their recollections cannot **be** otherwise than dim and uncertain. But **the** achievements of Burton **in** Chambers Street ; the unexampled popularity of his theatre ; the unequalled company he gathered there ; the indisputable creations of **character that** there originated ; the birth of **a** revival of Shakespeare, with a felicity **of** conception that revealed the appreciative student, and **with a beauty and** minuteness of appointment unprecedented at the time ;—all this, through a decade of years, forms an enchanting reminiscence vivid still in the retrospect of numberless New Yorkers. **It** is not surprising that we of the **city of New** York forget that the comedian so long belonged to Philadelphia.

So brilliant was his success in Chambers Street that all other theatres where he flourished seem **to be** viewed by the reflected light of that ; and we think **there** will be no question that there **were** clustered his rarest triumphs and **there** blossomed the flower of his fame.

BURTON'S THEATRE,

CHAMBERS STREET.

———

" There is the playhouse now, there must you sit."

—Shakespeare.

31

1848–1856.

PALMO'S **Opera-House was built in** 1842, and, according **to** Wemyss' Chronology, was the sixteenth theatre erected in **New York. It was** built by Ferdinand Palmo, and designed for the presentation **of** Italian opera. **To** Palmo, it is said, belongs the honor **of** having first introduced that department of music in the city. **In** 1844 he opened with " Lucia di Lammermoor "; **but the** support given to his venture was no**t** generous, notwithstanding the fact that wealth and fashion still resided in Warren, Murray, and Beekman streets. **The** time apparently was not ripe ; the experiment ended in financial **ruin to** Palmo, and **the** unfortunate man **never** wholly recovered from the blow. The house passed into divers hands, and was the scene of **a** variety of entertain-

ments for two or three years afterward. The
writer remembers distinctly going there of an
afternoon, when a boy, to a circus entertainment. The place was at a low ebb in point of
popularity and attraction when the comedian
fixed upon it as his future professional home.
He rearranged, fitted it up, and adorned it, and
called it BURTON'S THEATRE.

It had no doubt long been a dream of the
manager to attain as nearly as possible to perfection in the organization and direction of a
first-class theatre. His varied experience in
Philadelphia and elsewhere constantly suggested an administration composed of members
equally valuable in their respective lines, and
forming an harmonious whole under an efficient
executive, as the best system of government
for the growth and development of dramatic
art ; and perhaps during his reign in Chambers
Street he came as near the realization of that
dream as is permitted to human aspiration. In
confirmation of the foregoing, we quote a passage from William B. Wood's Recollections,

Palmo's Opera-House, afterward Burton's Theatre. (After a water-color drawing in the collection of Thomas J. McKee, Esq.)

where, writing in 1854 of the evils of the star system, he says : " Let me here remark, that I am happy to see of late times—I mean within the last few years—that the pernicious system of which I speak, by carrying itself fairly out, and by so breaking up all sound stock companies, has finally destroyed itself. * * * To that intelligent manager, Mr. Burton, the first credit is due. He has been striving for a number of years in New York, as he had been doing here in Philadelphia, to bring his theatre to a proper system, based on the principles of common sense and experience. With talents of his own equalled by few stars, he has preferred to ascertain whether the public could, not be better attracted by a good stock company of combined talent, and every New Yorker knows with what excellent effect he has labored. His success, I am happy to learn, has amply confirmed his reputation for dramatic judgment."

We may supplement this by a paragraph taken from Laurence Hutton's entertaining

volume of " Plays and Players." Describing in
glowing terms the production of Buckstone's
comedy of " Leap Year," at Burton's, March 1,
1850, **Mr.** Hutton says : " That our readers
may fully comprehend the subject and period
of which we write, it will be well to remind
them, perhaps, **that the** art of acting had
arrived at such a point in Burton's Theatre,
that, to play a comedy well, was not enough.
Every thing was so well done, so perfect in
every respect, mere excellence **was** so much a
matter of course, was so positive, **on** the
Chambers Street boards, **that** there **was** but
little room for the comparative, and the
superlative **itself was** necessary to create a
sensation."

The Chambers Street Theatre opened July
10, 1848, with " Maidens, **Beware** "; " Raising
the Wind," **and " The** Irish Dragoon." These
were succeeded **by " New** York in Slices,"
" **Dan** Keyser **de** Bassoon," and " Lucy Did
Sham Amour." The work **was slow at** first,
but the disappearance of money was rapid.

We have seen, however, that there was no
limit to Burton's energy and perseverance.
He played in New York, Philadelphia, and
Baltimore, week after week ; managed, in conjunction with John Brougham, an engagement
with Mr. W. C. Macready at Ford's Theatre,
Boston, October, 1848 ; was announced, on
Macready's departure, to appear himself ; but
the intention was unfulfilled, and so it
chanced that he never acted there until the
last years of his life. He played for the
benefit of the widow and family of Edmund Simpson, at the Park Theatre, December 7, 1848, in referring to which event
Mr. Ireland says : "We insert the entire
bill to show the forgetfulness of self evinced
by the volunteers, and their willingness to
assume any character to insure the best result, there being no less than five gentlemen
in the cast who had played, and might justly
have laid claim to the principal character of
the play." The play was "The School for
Scandal," cast principally as follows :

SIR PETER TEAZLE . .	Mr. HENRY PLACIDE.
SIR OLIVER SURFACE . .	" WM. E. BURTON.
JOSEPH SURFACE . . .	" THOMAS BARRY.
CHARLES SURFACE . .	" GEORGE BARRETT.
CRABTREE	" W. R. BLAKE.
SIR BENJAMIN BACKBITE .	" PETER RICHINGS.
CARELESS . . .	" C. M. WALCOT.
SIR HARRY . . .	" H. HUNT.
MOSES . . .	" JOHN POVEY.
TRIP	" DAWSON.
LADY TEAZLE .	Mrs. SHAW.
LADY SNEERWELL	" JOHN GILBERT.
MRS. CANDOUR	" WINSTANLEY.
MARIA . .	Miss MARY TAYLOR.

This deed of charity was followed by others
for the same object on the part of New York
managers, and among them Burton contributed
a night at his own theatre, on the 5th of March
ensuing, in which the full strength of his company appeared.

The burning **of the** Park Theatre in 1848
left Burton without **a** rival. The Olympic was
of the past; Forrest thundered at the Broadway; Wallack's and Daly's were yet to be. It
was not long before the public discovered the
genius that presided in Chambers Street, and
recognized the unusual excellence which char-

acterized the performances. The location **was**
favorable for **Brooklyn** people, and from first
to last the theatre enjoyed a monopoly of their
patronage. " **For** several years," says Ireland,
" Burton's **Theatre was the** resort of the most
intelligent **class of** pleasure-seekers, and there
beauty, wit, and fashion, loved **to** congregate,
without the formality **or etiquette of** attire
once deemed necessary at the **Park."** Its fame
was really phenomenal. Leaping metropolitan
bounds, it spread to **distant** states and neighborhoods, and became, one might almost say,
a familiar **and** welcome **contribution to the**
social **and** intellectual communion of the time.
For a stranger to **come to New York** in those
days and omit **to visit Burton's,** would imply
an obtuseness so forlorn, or **an** indifference so
stolid, that **in the one** case he would be an
object of compassion, and in the other a grave
offender of public sentiment. But in all proba-
bility he looked forward during his journey
city-ward **to** his evening in those halls **of**
Momus ; **and** we may be certain that **the**

" Quips, and cranks, and wanton wiles,
Nods, and becks, and wreathèd smiles "

of that night lived in his memory for many a
long day.

It is not too much to say that this attraction was almost wholly due to the extraordinary powers of Burton himself. True, his
company embraced the finest artists in their
several lines of any stage in the country ; and
it was well known to all lovers of refined drama
that the Chambers Street Theatre was the
home of English comedy, and that any given
play could be there produced with a cast entirely adequate, and with a perfection of detail
ensuring to the auditor an artistic delight and
a representation of the highest class. But
there are many who, while appreciating the
delineation of manners and character, seek
amusement pure and simple, and who believe
that good digestion waits on hearty laughter.
To this large constituency Burton was the ob-
jective point, for his humor and comic power
were a perennial fountain of mirth. His ap-

pearance, either discovered when the **curtain
rose,** or entering from **the** wing, was the signal
for a ripple of merriment all over the house.
Every countenance brightened, the dullest
face glowed **with** gleeful expectancy. **No**
actor, we believe—unless possibly Liston,—
ever excelled **Burton** in humorous facial expression. **Tom Hood, in** referring to certain
pastimes of **a London evening, says in his**
felicitous rhyme :

> " Or in the small Olympic pit sit, **split,**
>   **Laughing at** Liston, while you **quiz his phiz.**"

Read the couplet thus :

> " Or in the *Chambers Street* snug pit sit, split,
>   Laughing at *Burton*, while you quiz his **phiz,**"

and we have the nightly situation. **It was a**
common circumstance for the theatre to receive
accessions toward the close of the performance,
the new-comers standing in line along the walls,
drawn thither by the potent magnet of the
manager in the farce. Thus it was that, though
the theatre furnished constantly **a** rich feast of

comedy, and was more widely known than any
other, still more celebrated was the great actor
whose name it bore; and it was the magic of
that name that drew the people, and it was he
whom the people went to see. It seemed to
make little difference what the bills announced;
Burton would play,—and that was enough.

It was the privilege **of** the writer of these
pages to have **free** access to the Chambers
Street Theatre, and to know personally its
manager, and his recollections are such as to
induce him to believe that in no better way can
he perform his task of completing Mr. Burton's
career than by employing his own knowledge
and recording the impressions he received. **In**
so doing, the opportunity afforded for special
reference **to members of** his company will be
improved; and perhaps our retrospection may
arouse **in** other breasts a remembrance of past
delight.

Alluding to the comedian's first appearance
in New York, October 31, 1837, Joseph N. Ireland, so often quoted, remarks: "The advent

of Mr. W. E. Burton, the most renowned comedian of recent days, demands more than a passing notice. For nearly twenty years no other
actor monopolized so much of the public
applause, and popular sentiment universally
assigned him a position in broad low comedy
entirely unrivalled on the American stage." It
was a little over three years between his arrival
in America and his New York début; about
eleven between that appearance and his lesseeship in Chambers Street; and eleven more
remain to be taken note of. Of these, eight
belong to Chambers Street, two to the uptown
theatre, and one to starring engagements in
various cities—the last being in Hamilton,
Canada, and abruptly terminated by the mala-
dy of which he died.

————

The company at Chambers Street now demands our attention ; and the wish to suitably
recognize the talents, and to chronicle, however
simply, the triumphs of that famous array, has
constrained us to widen the scope of our origi-

nal design, and to extend somewhat our notices **of** certain individual actors. We shall **in** nowise regret this; for in recalling past delight it is a pleasure to dwell on those who caused it; **and** we may, perchance, awaken thereby a happy thought **of** them in other hearts. The **departed** years are full of memories, and the turning of a leaf **may lay** bare a volume of reminiscence. **It** forms no part of our purpose, however, to follow individual careers, and to trace their course on other boards than those of the Chambers Street Theatre. Many of them, indeed, after Burton removed uptown, and after his death, continued their successes and won renown in other scenes and under other management; and our readers may feel that but scant justice is done many meritorious names famil-**iar to the present** generation, **in** confining mention of them to a period when their talents and capabilities had not ripened to that excellence which afterward gave them fame. But we are concerned with them only as they figured **as** members of Burton's company, and as such

contributed **richly to our** fund **of** memory.
They stand **in the** dramatic Pantheon **with**
their great chief; and in approaching that
central and dominant **figure we** pause **to**
bend delighted **gaze upon the** admirable group
surrounding it.

From 1848 to 1856 the following names were
numbered on the muster-roll: Henry Placide,
Blake, **Brougham, Lester, T. B.** Johnston, Bland,
Jordan, Barrett, Dyott, Fisher, Thompson, Holland, **C. W. Clarke, Norton,** Parsloe, **Jr., Hol-**
man, Charles Mathews, Setchell, Mrs. Hughes,
Mrs. Russell **(now Mrs. Hoey),** Mrs. Skerrett,
Mrs. Rea, Miss Raymond, Mrs. Hough, Mrs.
Buckland, Miss Weston, **Miss** Devlin, Miss
Malvina, Miss Agnes Robertson, **Fanny** Wallack, Mary Taylor, Miss Chapman. This is
by no means intended as a complete enumera-
tion—"**but** 't is enough, 't will serve." Many
names have been forgotten, and some remembered but omitted. It may **be of** interest to
note at this point the fortunes that awaited
at least five **of** the actresses above named—

viz.: **Mrs. Russell,** Miss **Weston, Miss** Devlin, **Miss** Malvina, **Miss Agnes Robertson.**

Mrs. Russell, while at **Burton's in** 1849, **and a** great **favorite, was married to John Hoey of express fame, and shortly** thereafter retired **from the stage, the manager** doing the honors **at her farewell, and** presenting **her on** the oc- **casion with a valuable** testimonial of his regard. **Long afterward** Mrs. **H**oey was induced by the **elder Wallack to forsake her retirement,** and **for many years was the leading lady at** his **theatre, her refined manners, correct** taste, and **exquisite toilets,** exciting **anew public** esteem **and admiration. She quitted the stage and returned to private life in** 1865.

Miss Lizzie Weston, whose beauty, dramatic aptitude, and versatility, won nightly plaudits, **and whose** performance was not without much **that was highly meritorious,** signalized **a** career **more or less checkered by** uniting her fortunes **with those of the late Charles** Mathews, during **his starring tour in** 1858, **and is now the widow of that famous actor.**

Miss Malvina, a sister of Mrs. Barney Williams, was a *danseuse* at Burton's,—for it was the fashion in the old days to beguile the lazy time between the pieces with a Terpsichorean interlude; and we remember but one instance of her appearance in any other character, and that was a minor part in the farce of "A School for Tigers." She became Mrs. Wm. J. Florence in 1853, and has since shared her husband's fortunes and honors. Miss Agnes Robertson made her début in New York at the Chambers Street Theatre, October 22, 1853, as *Milly* in "The Young Actress," and has since been well known as the wife of Dion Boucicault.

A more illustrious alliance—so soon to end in piteous sorrow—was the portion of Mary Devlin. She was a minor actress at Burton's, but a woman of rare and lovely character. So much so, that she won the heart of Edwin Booth, and became his wife, and the idol of his home, till death early called her from his side. It was in memory of this sweet and gentle lady, that the poet Thomas William Parsons penned the following exquisite stanzas:

" What shall we do now, Mary being dead,
 Or say, or write, that shall express the half ?
What can we do but pillow that fair head
 And let the spring-time write her epitaph ?

" **As it** will soon in snow-drop, violet,
 Wind-flower, and columbine, and maiden's tear,—
Each letter of that pretty alphabet
 That spells in flowers the pageant of the year.

" She was a maiden for **a man to** love,
 She was a woman for a husband's life,
One that had learned to value far above
 The name of Love the sacred name **of** Wife.

" Her little life-dream, rounded so with sleep,
 Had all there is of life—except gray hairs :
Hope, love, trust, passion, and devotion deep,
 And that mysterious tie a Mother bears.

" She hath fulfilled her promise and hath past :
 Set her down gently at the iron door !
Eyes ! look on that loved image for the **last :**
 Now cover it in earth—her earth no **more !** "

Let us now summon, as first in order, the
name that heads the list **of** the actors above
given. Henry Placide enjoyed in public estimation a fame worthy and well deserved. He
was an actor of the old school, and his conceptions were the fruit of appreciative and careful

study; his acting was a lucid and harmonious
interpretation of his author; and his elocution,
clear and resonant, was the speech of a scholar
and a gentleman. The artistic sense was never
forgotten in his delineations, and his name on
the bills was a guaranty of intellectual pleasure.
He was not broadly funny like Burton, or
Holland; but those who remember his *Sir
Harcourt Courtley*, his *Jean Jacques François
Antoine Hypolite de Frisac*, in "Paris and
London," and his *Clown*, in Shakespeare's
"Twelfth Night," will not deny that he was
the owner of a rich vein of eccentric humor,
and that he worked his possession effectually.
He was an expert in the Gallic parts where the
speech is a struggle between French and English, and, indeed, since his departure they, too,
have vanished from the stage. But those who
saw him as *Haversac*, in "The Old Guard";
as *The Tutor*, in "To Parents and Guardians";
or as *Monsieur Dufard*, in "The First Night,"
will bear witness to his inimitable manner, and
to his facile blending of the grave and gay.

We shall never forget how, in the last-named
character (*Mons. Dufard*), having engaged his
daughter for a " first appearance," and having
declared his own ability to manage the drum
in the orchestra on the occasion, he, suddenly,
during the mimic rehearsal, at an allusion in
the text to sunrise, stamped violently on the
stage ; and to the startled manager's exclama-
tion of " What 's that ! " serenely replied : " Zat
ees ze cannon vich announce ze brek of day—
I play him on ze big drum in ze night." In
choleric old men Placide was unsurpassed. All
the touches that go toward the creation of a
grim, irascible, thwarted, bluff old gentleman,
he commanded at will. His *Colonel Hardy*,
in " Paul Pry," for instance, what an example
was that ! I hear him, now, at the close of the
comedy, when things had drifted to a happy
anchorage—hear him saying in reply to the
soothing remark : " Why, Colonel, you 've
every thing your own way,"—" Yes, I know I
have every thing my own way ; but —— it, I
hav' n't *my own way* of having it ! " His rep-

ertory covered a wide range ; and we retain
vivid recollections of his *Sir Peter Teazle*, his
Doctor Ollapod, and his *Silky ;* the last in " The
Road to Ruin," in which comedy, by the way,
we remember seeing Placide, Blake, Burton,
Lester, Bland, and Mrs. Hughes ; truly a phenomenal cast.

Such, briefly sketched, was the actor who
constituted one of Burton's strongest pillars.
For some years he played at no other theatre
in New York. He gave enjoyment to thousands, and in dramatic annals his name and
achievements have distinguished and honorable
record. As one of the many who remain to
own their debt of pleasure and instruction,
the present writer pays this tribute to the
genius and memory of Henry Placide.[1]

We now summon another name from the
famous corps, for the purpose of analysis, since

[1] " When Edwin Forrest was in Europe on a visit, he was
asked whom he deemed the best American actor ; he promptly
and unequivocally replied : ' Henry Placide is unquestionably the best general actor on the American boards, and I
doubt whether his equal can be found in England.' "—HENRY
DICKINSON STONE'S " Theatrical Reminiscences."

we should be ill content with the cold respect
of a passing glance at an artist so celebrated
as was William **Rufus** Blake. **We** can recall
no actor of the past, and we know of but one
in the present, comparable with Blake in certain lines of old men—certainly in the rôle of
tender pathos like *Old Dornton*, and in the
portrayal of a sweetly noble nature framed in
venerable simplicity, as in *Jesse Rural*, he had
no equal; and it is simply truth to say that
with him departed from the stage that unique,
all-affecting, wondrous embodiment of *Geoffrey
Dale*, in " The Last Man."

The characteristics of Blake's power were a
broad heartiness, suggestive sentiment, and
eloquent idealization. These traits informed
respectively the parts he essayed, and gave to
each in turn rare flow of spirit, richness of
color, and poetic fervor. For the verbal expression of these salient elements, he pos-
sessed a tuneful voice, which rose or fell
as the sway of feeling dictated, and his delivery was singularly felicitous in tone and

emphasis. **Nor** was he lacking in a humor **at** once subtle **and** delicate, happily evinced **in** his acting of *Mr. Primrose*, in the comedietta of " Bachelors' **Torments."**

Those who saw Blake at **the period of which** we are writing, found **it hard to** believe **that** the *Sir Anthony Absolute* of aldermanic **pro-** portions before them was once a slender young man and played light comedy ! Yet so it **was.** Very old play-goers **will recollect** the Chatham Garden theatre, **and perhaps some** tenacious memory bears record of having seen Blake there **in** the long ago ; for **there he** first appeared to a New **York** audience, in 1824, playing *Frederick*, in Colman's " Poor Gentleman." We never saw him earlier than at Burton's, and then **with added** years had come **a** ro- tundity of person which, however unobjec- tionable **in the** famous impersonations of his prime, was not, it must be confessed, the ideal physique of light comedy ; so his *Frederick* had long departed and his *Sir Robert Bramble* had appeared.

The first time we saw Blake was in " The Road to Ruin," and the impression he made has never been effaced. We were young, it is true, and sentimental, and easily moved; but our heart tells us that the effect would be the same could we see the actor in the play to-morrow. We have read since of the extra-ordinary sensation produced by the great Mun-den in the part of *Old Dornton* ; but we have an abiding faith that the acting of the famous Englishman would have been no revelation to Blake ; and we cannot, indeed, conceive of any added touch that would not have impaired, rather than heightened, the latter's superb delineation. But Blake's portrayal of the out-raged, doting, fond, tender father, is, like his *Jesse* **Rural,** so fresh in the memory of living persons, that we feel it to be needless to des-cant upon its beauties. Few will forget the years of his last and long engagement at Wal-lack's—a fitting crown for a great artistic career. Blake played many parts and rarely touched but to adorn. Even his *Malvolio,* had it not

been for the advent of Charles Fisher (who was
born in yellow stockings and cross-gartered),
would have passed into history as a carefully
conceived and highly finished performance.
Whenever we see **Mr. John Gilbert we are re-**
minded of Blake. There is a grace of action, a
courtliness of manner, inseparable from **Gilbert,**
which lends **to all** his efforts **an elevating**
charm, a feature Blake did not possess **in like**
degree. **But the two** actors belonged to the
same school ; their traditions will be much
akin ; and neither loses **in** being spoken of **in**
the same breath, and with the same accent **of**
admiration.

Following Placide and Blake **is the** name of
an actor **better remembered than** either, **and**
whose death is **of comparatively recent** date.
We refer **to** John Brougham, who **for** thirty
years and more was one of New York's prime
favorites, and his name is associated with many
of the drama's brightest **and** worthiest triumphs. His inexhaustible **flow** of spirits, in
his best days, pervaded **all his** acting, and in-

vested the most unattractive part with an allur-
ing charm, as many a prosaic spot in nature
becomes enchanted land by the music of falling waters.   Add to this exuberant vitality a
rich endowment of mother wit ; a bright intelligence ; keen sympathy and appreciation, and
rare personal magnetism, and you have before
you " glorious John," whose hearty voice it
was always a pleasure to hear, and whose face,
beaming with humor, was always welcomed
with delight.

Brougham was Burton's stage manager in
1848, and his dramatization of " Dombey and
Son " was first produced in that year.   The
representation of this play established the
Chambers Street Theatre, drew attention to
the talents of the stock company, and put
money into Burton's purse.   If theatres, like
other things, succeed either by hook or crook,
as the saying is, surely it was by hook that the
manager won fame and fortune, for the digit of
Captain Cuttle held sway like a wizard's wand.
The temptation to dwell here on this renowned

MR. BURTON AS CAPTAIN CUTTLE

Burtonian impersonation is hard to resist ; but
we must be patient and bide our time.

Brougham played *Bunsby* and *Bagstock*, investing the oracular utterances of the tar, and
the roughness and toughness and " devilish "
slyness of the *Major*, with a humor and spirit
all his own. We laugh outright as we think
of that scene where *Cuttle* is being rapidly
reduced to agony and despair by *Mrs. Mac-
Stinger*, and is rescued therefrom by *Bunsby*,
who, with a hoarse " Avast, my lass ; avast ! "
advances solemnly on the redoubtable female,
and with a soothing gravity ejects the entire
MacStinger family, following in the rear himself
—*Cuttle* meanwhile gazing in speechless aston-
ishment at the unexpected succor, until the
door is closed ; and then, drawing an immense
breath, and turning toward the audience his
inimitable face, exclaims in a tone of profound
respect and admiration : " There 's wisdom ! "

It was a great treat to see Burton and
Brougham together. The two actors were so
ready, so full of wit, so alive to each other's

points and by-play, that any fanciful interpolation of the text, or humorous impromptu, by
the one, was instantly responded **to** by the
other ; and the house was often thrown into
convulsions of merriment by these purely un-
premeditated sallies. This was notably the
case in the afterpiece of " An Unwarrantable
Intrusion "—committed **by Mr.** Brougham upon Mr. Burton—when in the **tag** the comedians suddenly assumed their own persons, and,
addressing each other by their proper names,
engaged in **a** droll colloquy respecting the
dilemma of having nothing to say to conclude
the piece ; and each suggesting in turn **some-**
thing that ought to or might be said to an audience under such peculiar and distressing circumstances,—the audience meanwhile **in a state of**
hilarious excitement, drinking in every spark-
ling jest and repartee, **and** wishing the flow of
humor would last forever.

And here we are reminded of an incident not
down in the bills, **which** furnished an audience
with an unlooked-for and affecting episode. **It**

occurred during the performance of Colman's comedy of " John Bull," produced for the benefit of a favorite actor ; Burton playing *Job Thornberry*, and Brougham, who had volunteered for the occasion, appearing in his capital rôle of *Dennis Brulgruddery*. Brougham was no longer with Burton—an estrangement existed between them of which the public was aware —and the conjunction of the two actors naturally awakened a lively interest. It chances in the comedy that *Mary Thornberry* finds a refuge in her distress at the " Red Cow," and is greatly befriended by *Dennis*. Her father, discovering her there, and grateful for the service rendered, exclaims: " You have behaved like an emperor to her. Give me your hand, landlord ! " Now, in the play, the reply of *Dennis* is: " Behaved !—(*refusing his hand*)— Arrah, now, get away with your blarney,"—but Brougham paused for a moment before Burton's outstretched hand, and then, as if yielding to an impulse, stretched forth his, and the two actors stood with clasped hands amidst an

outburst of applause that fairly shook the
building. Of course they were "called out "
at the close, and Brougham, in the course of
a felicitous little speech, remarked—alluding,
perhaps, to the success of his Lyceum not
being all he could wish—that he had "lately
run off the track"; to which Burton, in his
turn, responded by saying : "Mr. Brougham
says he has 'run off the track.' Well, he *has*
run off the track ; but he has n't burst his boiler
yet ! " At this speech the enthusiasm of the
audience knew no bounds ; and indeed, with
the exception of Mary Taylor's farewell benefit,
we can recall no theatrical occasion where more
genuine feeling was manifested.

But to return to " Dombey and Son." **Mrs.**
Brougham was the original *Susan Nipper*, and
played the part acceptably ; but all previous
Nippers suffered eclipse when Caroline Chapman appeared at a later date, giving us a *Susan*
that seemed to have sprung full-*Nippered* from
the head of Boz himself. Her inimitable acting and ring of delivery were like a new light

turned on the scene. Her flow of spirit and
alert movement, her independent air and saucy
glance, her not-to-be-put-down-under-any-cir-
cumstances manner,—all was freshness and
sparkle, and her presence was as welcome to the
audience as a summer shower to drooping
wayside flowers. Miss Chapman was a great
acquisition to Burton's, and her bright individuality shone in all her assumptions. Her
line was the stage soubrette, a specialty which
she lifted entirely out of the commonplace and
informed it with force and distinction. It is a
pleasure to place on record the memory of
happy hours that we owe to the performances
of Caroline Chapman.

The original *Toots* was Oliver B. Raymond,
whom we never saw. T. B. Johnston was his
successor, and as that admirable comedian
never did any thing unacceptably, his *Toots*
was a memorable effort; and had *Uriah Heep*
not followed we should have been satisfied
with his *Toots;* but when "Copperfield" was
produced and Johnston appeared as *Heep*, it

seemed as if he was born for that and nothing
else.   Now that we think of it, it seems to us,
as we recall Johnston, that nature had peculiarly fitted him for the delineation of many of
Dickens's characters.   Something in his spare
figure, his grotesqueness of demeanor, his
whimsical aspect, his odd manner of speech,
continually suggested a flavor of Boz; and
whether as *Toots*, or *Heep*, or *Newman Noggs*, he
seemed to have glided into his element, and
was *en rapport* with the great novelist.

We must not forget, in writing of "Dombey
and Son," to note how much its attraction was
enhanced by the assumption, in 1849, of the
part of *Edith* by Mrs. Josephine Russell (the
present Mrs. Hoey).   Laurence Hutton, referring to the event in his volume of "Plays
and Players," says: "Up to the time of
her assumption of the rôle, *Edith*, in Brougham's version of the story, was comparatively
a secondary part, and one to which but
little attention had been paid either by per-
former or audience.   Mrs. Russell, however,

by her refined and elegant manner, brought
Edith and herself into favor and prominence.
She made of *Edith* more than Brougham himself ever imagined could be made ; and *Edith*
made her a reputation and a success on the
New York stage, which, until her honorable
and much-to-be-regretted retirement, she ever
sustained.[1]

We have dwelt thus on " Dombey and Son,"
because, in the first place, it gained for the
Chambers Street Theatre an enduring public
regard, and was no doubt the incentive to the
after-production of dramatizations of Dickens,
which gave us Burton in *Micawber, Squeers,
Mr. Bumble*, and *Sam Weller ;* and because in
so celebrating it we pay a deserved tribute to
Brougham, from whose fertile brain and ready
pen it came. We may say, in this connection,
that not only as actor, but as playwright also,
Brougham achieved fame and honor. Many
of his comedies are well known to the stage,

[1] The first appearance of Mrs. Russell (whose maiden name
was Shaw) in Chambers Street was made September 3, 1849.

and are included **in** the published drama ; and
as a writer of burlesque we question whether
any thing better or funnier than his "Po-
ca-hon-tas or the Gentle Savage" has ever
been composed.   Of one thing we are certain :
an incarnate pun-fiend presided over its creation.
This' extravaganza, first acted at Wallack's
Lyceum, took the town by storm, and its bons-
mots, **local** hits, and trenchant witticisms, were
on the lips of everybody.   In structure, idea,
and treatment of theme, it was ludicrous to a
degree.   **Who does not** remember Brougham
and the late Charles Walcot in their respective
parts of *Powhattan* and *Captain Smith ?*

It goes without saying that Brougham's
Hibernian delineations were perfect and to the
manner born.   Many an Irish farce we recall,
during his stay at **Burton's, to** which he gave a
new lease of life ; and we congratulate ourselves that our memory holds record of having
once seen **him** as *Sir Lucius O'Trigger*, the
only cast in our experience wherein Sheridan's
creation found a fitting representative.

We now pause before an actor of illustrious
lineage ; **of a** name honored in dramatic annals
by encomiums bestowed only upon abilities **of**
the highest **order; an actor who,** conscious
of his inheritance of **genius, worthily** perpetu-
ates the traditions of his house ; and **who is
now,** despite the flight of time, the most engaging and accomplished comedian known to the
American stage. Our readers will need **no**
further introduction **to** Lester Wallack, the
" Mr. Lester " of Burton's, where first we saw
him so many **years ago.** We recall the evening when we sat in the cosy parquette, awaiting
with eager interest the **rising of the** curtain on
Charles Dance's comic **drama of** " Delicate
Ground," in which **Mr.** Lester would make his
" first appearance since his return from England " (so the bill ran), in the character **of**
Citizen Sangfroid. We say eager interest, for
we had heard much **of Mr.** Lester : that he
was graceful, handsome, *distingué,*—in fact,
splendid generally ; and **our** expectancy was
akin to that of the watching astronomer—

" When a new planet swims into his ken."

At last the tinkle of the bell; the curtain rose, and enter Miss Mary Taylor, the universal favorite, as *Pauline.* Her soliloquy closes with the cue for *Sangfroid's* entrance, and at the words, " Hush ! my husband ! " a pause succeeded—and then from " door left " was protruded an elegantly booted foot, and a moment later Lester stood before us, bowing with characteristic ease and grace to the demonstrations of welcome. We confess to an unconditional surrender on that occasion. The actual fact was far beyond any expectation or hope. We thought we had never seen any one quite so splendid ; and *Sangfroid* was forthwith invested with the best and noblest elements that combine to elevate mankind. We endeavored for many days afterward to conform our daily life to the general teachings of *Sangfroid;* we imitated the gait and manner, the calm aplomb of *Sangfroid;* the accent of *Sangfroid* was impressed on all our ordinary forms of speech ; our conversation on whatever topic was plentifully sprinkled with *Sangfroidisms;* in short, the whole tenor of our existence was shaped and directed by *Sangfroid* in the person of Mr. Lester. We recovered in due course from our abject submission to the spell of *Sangfroid;* but Lester continued to stretch forth the " sceptre of fascination," and to his matchless grace and finish we owe many a delightful recollection.

Then in early manhood,[1] the unrestrained alertness and vivacity of youth were his in bounteous measure. He was in the *Percy Ardent* and *Young Rapid* period, and had not yet entered the corridor of years at the far end of which lurked the *blasé* figure of " My Awful Dad." We remember him in so many parts which in all likelihood he never will play again ! There was *Rover*, in " Wild Oats," that buskined hero, with his captivating nonchalance dashed with tragic fire ; his tender conversion of *Lady Amaranth*—played, be it said, with all proper

[1] Lester Wallack's first appearance in New York was made at the Broadway Theatre, Sept. 27, 1847, as *Sir Charles Coldstream* in " Used Up."

demureness **by** Miss Lizzie Weston; his **tri-**
umph **over** *Ephraim Smooth*—one of Blake's
instances of versatility—in a scene rich with
the spirit of frolic abandon ; and his humorous
tilt with *Sir George Thunder*—a belligerent
sea-dog, played by Burton as he alone could
play it—an episode replete with comic power ;
—**all** these contributed to a performance which
we revelled in many and many a night ; and
the memory of **it,** now as **we** write, draws near
in a succession of vivid pictures. There was
Tangent, in " The **Way** to Get Married," a
capital part in Lester's hands, blending manly
action and debonair grace with that easy transition to airy farcical expression, **a** favorite and
effective dramatic habit of this actor, and given
full play in **that** memorable prison scene in the
comedy, when, a victim **to** adverse circumstances, **and** actually fettered, he makes felicitous use **of his** handkerchief to hide his mortification **and his** chains from the eyes of the
heroine during her visit **of** sympathy. *Percy*
Ardent, in " The **West End," was another of**

his **characteristic** assumptions in those days;
so also **were** *Young Rapid*, in "A Cure for the
Heartache," **and the** *Hon. Tom Shuffleton*, in
"John **Bull**"; and, **indeed**, Burton's frequent
revivals of the **old** comedies would have been a
difficult matter without **Lester; for** in every
one of them a light comedy part is distinctly
drawn, and unquestionably **the** rarest among
all dramatic artists **is the** first-class **light**
comedian.

Let **any one** who thinks **otherwise** endeavor
to recall the names of those who have been **or**
are famous in that special line, and he will be
surprised **to** find how few he can enumerate.
One might suppose that all young actors would
naturally incline toward light comedy, **and be**
ambitious in that direction, since in that sphere
are found the charm **of** youth, the expression
of lofty sentiment, the impulse **to** chivalrous
action, the opportunity for the display **of**
graceful and manly bearing,—not to mention
the lover, whom, as Emerson declares, all the
world loves: and why **then,** one may **ask,**

should there not be always a plentiful crop of
ripening light comedians? Alas, **it** is not
enough to be young, good-looking, intelligent,
and of virtuous impulse, **or** even **a** lover.
Something more **is** needed, and **we** conceive
it to be that gift of nature, which study and
practice **develop into** seeming perfect art, but
which **neither** study nor practice can create;
the gift, **let us say, of** perceiving instinctively
the salient points of **a** character, and going beyond **the** author in felicitous and suggestive
expression of them. It is easier, we think, to
compass tragedy; **easier to** simulate age;
easier to be funny; than to **be at** once airy
and gay, delicately humorous, and engagingly
manly. There are fewer light comedians
born,—that is the whole story; and where we
find one actor like Lester Wallack, we meet
with plenty of **every other** specialty. This
was made strikingly evident by Burton's experi-
ments **in** supplying Lester's place, when the
latter joined his father in the establishment of
Wallack's **Lyceum. Charles** Fisher was im-

ported, and he for a season essayed to succeed
Lester ; but

"The expectancy and rose of the fair state"

he was not, and it was not long before the
fiddle of *Triplet* and the yellow stockings of
Malvolio emancipated him from the bondage
of light comedy, revealed his true powers, and
made us grateful to Burton for introducing to
New York one of the best eccentric comedians
of the day. Dyott, Norton, and even Holman,
were severally thrown into the breach, such
was the strait in which the manager found
himself ; and it was not until he secured George
Jordan that equilibrium was restored to the
company.

But to return. The versatility of Lester, so
conspicuous throughout his career, was early
made apparent. We remember him as *Steer-
forth*, as *Sir Andrew Aguecheek*, and *Captain
Murphy Maguire ;* and though in the last he
acted under the shadow of Brougham's rich
impersonation, still he was a delightful *Captain.* We saw him as the young lover, in

" Paul Pry " ; as *Frederick*, in " The Poor Gentleman," and many more ; besides those parts,
such as *Young Marlow*, *Charles Surface*, and
Captain Absolute, which need no reference,
since they remain ripe and finished conceptions in his present repertory.   But **of** all his
delineations of **the past,** that which we linger
on with the greatest pleasure, and which
affected us most, was his *Harry Dornton*, in
" The Road to Ruin."   From the moment he
appears beneath his father's window, importu-
nate for admittance, he awakens an interest
and sympathy that follow him **to** the end.
The part abounds in touches of Lesterian hue
and flavor : the **scene** just mentioned ; that
wherein *Milford* makes careless and heartless
allusion to *Old Dornton*, and is met by *Harry's*
eloquent **and** electric **rebuke** ; the scene with
the *Widow Warren*, and with *Sophia* ;—all are
charming ; **and** we feel it to be no small tribute
to hold in memory Lester's *Harry* side by side
with the *Old Dornton* **of** Blake.

   We have spoken **of T. B.** Johnston, and re-

ferred to famous **parts of** his, particularly **to**
the conception and **execution of certain** characters in Dickens which undeniably **he** made
his own; but we remember **this actor in** other
and sundry enjoyable delineations, of which
brief mention may be made. The odd aspect
of Johnston, joined to his whimsical method,
so **in** keeping, **as** before remarked, **with** the
creations of Boz, peculiarly fitted him for the
apt portrayal **of** those idiosyncrasies of **nature
and** temperament shadowed forth by characters
in many of the old farces, in which he **often
appeared,** those pieces being quite the fashion
in the **days of which we are** writing. **We may**
instance *Panels,* in **" A School for** Tigers," **as**
one of these; his part **in "** A Blighted Being "
(the **name** quite forgotten), was another;
Humphrey Dobbins, in " The Poor Gentleman "
(that not a farce, **however),** was a capital **por-**
traiture, and an amusing **foil to** Burton's *Sir*
***Robert** Bramble;* his *Miss Smithers,* in **" A**
Thousand Milliners," **where he** almost divided
the honors with Burton as *Madam Vander-*

pants ;—these are **a few** of the many that come
floating back on the tide of recollection.

Bland was a useful member of Burton's
company, though we think his stay was brief,
and he contributes less to memory, as it
chances, than many others. We never regard-
ed him as a great actor, though we have read
of his being thought the best *Jacques* of **his**
day, and very fine as *Sir Thomas Clifford.* We
never saw him in either, and have no recollection **of** "The Hunchback" being produced at
the Chambers Street Theatre. **In** "The Honey-
moon" Burton himself **was** the *Jacques.*
We remember Bland very well as *Sulky,* in
"The Road to Ruin," and as *Ham,* in "David
Copperfield," **and** both efforts were creditable
and contributed to the general success—his
share in the exciting and touching scenes between *Old Dornton* and himself, as *Sulky,* being
admirably done.

We are surprised that we remember so little
interesting **to** record **of** Jordan. Succeeding
Lester, and deemed by many the peer of that

comedian, one might naturally suppose that his achievements **would** figure largely **in** these reminiscences; but **we** can recall **very few** impersonations of which we retain a vivid impression. We cannot concur with that estimate of his **powers** which ranked him with **Lester, yet we cordially admit** that he came **nearer than** any actor we **know** of. **He was** very handsome, had a fine stage presence, and was agreeable in all that he did. We recall his spirited performance **of** *Rover;* his *Kitely,* in Ben Jonson's "Every Man **in His** Humor"; his *Ferdinand,* in "The **Tempest**"; his *Lysander,* in "Midsummer Night's **Dream**"; and his *Captain Hawksley,* in "Still Waters **Run** Deep," was superb **and unequalled.** It was always a pleasure **to see** Jordan, and **we** owe to his acting many an hour of enjoyment.

George Barrett—or, "Gentleman George," as he **was** quite **as** well known—was one **of** Burton's company **for a** short period, and with his name are associated many pleasant memories. Among them we may mention with de-

light his performance of *Sir Andrew Aguecheek*, a companion picture to Fisher's *Malvolio*. His long body and attenuated "make
up," his piping voice, his fantastic manner,
and absurd assumption of acumen,—all contributed to an embodiment artistic and entertaining in the highest degree. He also played
Flute, the Bellows-Mender, in the revival of
" Midsummer Night's Dream " ; and it seems
but yesterday, so vivid is the remembrance,
that we saw him stalking about the stage, in
the guise of Ben Jonson's bombastic hero,
Captain Bobadil.

Old play-goers, if they remember nothing
else of John Dyott, will recollect his admirable reading—his distinct utterance—his
fine emphasis,—qualities specially noticeable in
his Shakespearian assumptions and in characters of a didactic cast ; and which made accepta-
ble many a part he undertook, half redeeming
it from deficiencies consequent upon natural
unfitness. It was such a pleasure to listen to
his delivery of the text, that you overlooked or

pardoned inadequacy of treatment in other respects. Necessarily his impersonations were
of very unequal merit. Certain phases of the
character assumed might be justly conceived
and well executed; others manifestly lacking
in the expression of what was naturally suggested, or sufficiently obvious. We might cite
instances of this—*Claude Melnotte* or *Alfred
Evelyn*, for example; but we prefer to think of
him in his most agreeable aspects, which were
not conspicuous in light comedy, though that
rôle, under the stress of exigency, often fell to
his lot.

We pleasantly recall him as *Lieut. Worthington*, in "The Poor Gentleman"; as *Pere-
grine*, in "John Bull"; as *Penruddoch*, in
"The Wheel of Fortune"; as *Duke Orsino*,
in "Twelfth Night"; as *Master Ford*, in
"The Merry Wives of Windsor"; and others
that might be mentioned. He was a useful
member of the Chambers Street company,
acted always with intelligence and spirit, and,
though leaving no great name, deserves re-

membrance as a finished reader and conscientious artist.

Charles Fisher, well known to the present
generation of play-goers as a sterling comedian,
came to Burton's after Lester's withdrawal,
and, as previously remarked, succeeded that
actor as the exponent of light comedy. We
saw him in several characters of that order;
but it must be confessed that his efforts, however praiseworthy, were not such as to induce
a condition of complacency on the part of the
management, with regard to his capacity in
that direction. But the whirligig of time, as
Shakespeare tells us, brings on its revenges;
and in due course Mr. Fisher had his, and a
truly artistic one it was.

It came about on the second revival of
"Twelfth Night," and was achieved in the
part of *Malvolio*. In referring to Blake's assumption of this character, we observed, in
passing, that Fisher was born in yellow stockings and cross-gartered—meaning to express
the natural affinity for Shakespeare's creation

existing in the actor; and we believe there
will be no question among those who remember the impersonation, as to the subtlety of
conception, the felicity of portrayal, and fidelity
to detail, that so eminently distinguished it.
From first to last it was a masterpiece. His
manner when he interrupts the orgies of *Sir
Toby*, the *Clown*, and *Aguecheek*, and during
their maudlin mockery, was full of rare suggestiveness; the great scene in the garden,
where he falls into the trap set by *Maria*, was
one of the finest pieces of acting known to our
stage. The audience were as intent during
its progress as if their own lives and fortunes
hung upon that enigmatic letter. When it
comes home to him at last that he indeed is
the favored of *Olivia*, and he gives full rein to
his fancy respecting his future exaltation—
how he must bear himself, the lofty air he will
assume, the consideration he will extort,—he
was inimitable. Already he is clothed in yellow stockings and cross-gartered; and he
smiles, as he struts, the smile that his de-

ceiver declares so becomes **him.**   In the ensuing scene before *Olivia*, where the stockings
and smiles play so important a **part, he** was
equally fine ; and if Fisher had played nothing
else, his *Malvolio* would **remain** an interpretation **of the** highest class, **and a** glory **of dra-**
matic art.   The press, with one accord, united
in its praise ; **and Mr.** Richard Grant White,
whose ability **to** judge of Shakespearian **de-**
lineations was well **known,** confessed, in **the**
columns **of the** *Courier and* *Inquirer* that he
did not know where Mr. Fisher learned to
play *Malvolio* **so well. To** say that we enjoyed
what we have here endeavored to recall, is to
say but little.   It is one of our most valued
memories—and we **could** not help thinking,
when the lovely *Viola* **of** the late Miss Neilson
was captivating all hearts, **what a** revelation it
would have been to **her** admiring audience had
Fisher presented his picture of *Malvolio.*

In **Burton's** revival **of** the " Midsummer
Night's Dream," **Fisher was cast** as *Duke The-*
seus ; **and in** thinking **of the part,** that glorious

passage descriptive of the *Duke's* hounds rings
in our ears, as spoken with glowing enthusiasm by the actor :

> " My hounds are bred out of the Spartan kind,
> So flew'd, so sanded ; and their heads are hung
> With ears that sweep away the morning dew ;
> Crook-kneed, and dew-lapp'd like Thessalian bulls ;
> Slow in pursuit, but match'd in mouth like bells,
> Each under each. A cry more tunable
> Was never holloa'd to, nor cheered with horn,
> In Crete, in Sparta, nor in Thessaly :
> Judge when you hear."

In "The Tempest" also, as *Prospero*, Mr.
Fisher appeared to advantage, and swayed the
destinies of the Enchanted Isle with dignity
and effect. *Triplet*, in "Masks and Faces,"
was another performance of Fisher's that we
might linger over in pleasant memory of its
humor and pathos ; a performance, too, by the
way, which brought to public view a new
accomplishment of the actor ; namely, his acquaintance with the violin,—an advantage that
lent unusual force and brilliancy to the capital
scene where *Woffington,* having played Lady
Bountiful to the forlorn family, completes her

conquest by calling for the fiddle and dancing "Cover the Buckle." And with the tune in our ears, and a vision of Fisher's elbow in deft movement, we take leave of the actor who gave us in the past so many happy hours.

An artist of quite another sort was Lysander Steele Thompson. He was an importation of Burton's; and his specialty was the Yorkshireman of the stage, a line in which he stood alone and unapproachable. Actors there have been who played the same parts, and with a sufficient mastery of the dialect to pass muster; but, compared with Thompson's, their assumptions were like artificial flowers in a painted vase beside a clump of spring violets in the dew of morning. The semblance was there; but the delicious fragrance of nature's breath it was not theirs to give. The native freshness and out-of-door breezy spirit were Thompson's own and born with him. His engagement was followed by the production of all the known plays in which there was a *Zekiel Homespun*, or a *Robin Roughhead*. We saw him in them all:

Bob Tyke, in " The School of Reform " ; *Zekiel Homespun*, in " The Heir-at-Law " ; *Stephen Harrowby*, in " The Poor Gentleman,"—and until the **advent of** Thompson, the *Harrowby* family had been **omitted in Burton's version of** the comedy ;—*Robin* **Roughhead**, in " A Plough- man Turned **Lord** " ; *John Browdie*, in " Nicho- las **Nickleby** " ; and *Giles*, in " The Miller's **Maid** " ; in which last, indeed, he **acted under an** inspiration that almost laid claim to genius itself ; **and** we see him now, **in that** high-wrought scene, where, **as** the defender **of virtue and** innocence, he towers **in** superb **wrath above** the villain *Gamekeeper*, **who would** tear **from** her home the person of *Susan Fellows.*

It goes without saying that his dialect was perfect, and **all the** humorous phases—the touches of bewilderment and arch simplicity, **the** quaint retort, the rollicking drollery, the innocence blent with audacity,—all these traits and characteristics **were so many** gifts of ex- pression summoned and employed at will. We **have** seen many tragedians and artists in melo-

drama ; many " old men " and light comedians ;
many funny **men** and eccentric actors, but we
have seen one Yorkshireman only—Lysander
Thompson.

He was not without vanity, however, and
possibly aspired to other dramatic walks than
his famous specialty, **if we** may judge from **a**
little episode in his career at Burton's, which
really makes too good a story to be lost.   Burton had in view the production of " The Merry
Wives," in order to act *Falstaff ;* and in the
distribution Thompson was asked to make
choice of a part.   The story runs that, after
due reflection, Mr. Thompson answered that on
the whole he would prefer to play *Sir John.*
The manager regarded him for a moment with
a glance **of** wonder, and then : " I'm —— if
you **do ;** one *Falstaff* is enough ; you must
choose again, Thompson."   And he chose the
*Host of the Garter **Inn**,* **and** made a palpable
hit.

The late Charles Mathews played a short en-
gagement at Burton's ; and we remember his

capital acting in " **Little** Toddlekins " and as *Young Rapid ;* but **we** need not dwell upon an actor whose stay was so fleeting, **whose** celebrity was so extended, and whose Memoirs **have** so recently been given to the public.

George Holland, also **departed, was for a** brief period at the Chambers Street **Theatre,** and **we** recall our enjoyment **of** his broad **fun** and facial extravagance. We **always felt, how-** ever, that—as his line was somewhat akin **to** Burton's—he underwent **a** perilous ordeal **in** appearing **on** the same stage with the **great** actor whose genius was **so** overshadowing.

Messrs. **Norton,**[1] Holman, **and Parsloe, jr.,**

---

[1] An amusing experience may be related apropos of Mr. Norton. Not liking a part in which he was cast, he addressed the following **letter to** the manager :

" MR. BURTON, My Dear Sir :—It was not necessity **which** drove me to America. I wished to travel, to see the country, and, after having satisfied myself as to whether it pleased me, professionally or otherwise, to arrange either to remain in it or return to England. I consider myself greatly insulted by being cast for the part of Scaley in ' Nicholas Nickleby. ' To offer such an indignity to a gentleman who **has** held **a** good position in the Olympic Theatre, London, under the management of so great an actor as Mr. W. Farren, where he has played Sir John Melville, Sir Lucius O'Trigger, Sir Arthur Lascelles, etc , I consider a great insult, and positively request

were useful members of the stock company,
limited in range and ability; and **we** mention
them as painstaking actors, **who** always did
their best, and aided materially in the general
success of the theatre. The name of young
Parsloe is included on account **of** his performance of *Puck,* which, owing **to** natural clever-
ness and acrobatic aptitude, he succeeded, **under Burton's** training, in making exceedingly
effective and full of goblin action.

And now let us fancy ourselves sitting, as **of**
old, in the parquette, the curtain having risen

you to take me out of the objectionable cast, and in future to
keep to the promise you made on engaging
            "Yours,   W. H. NORTON."

Shortly he received the following reply :

"MY DEAR MR. NORTON :—When I engaged you I thought
you were merely an actor. I find that you are a gentleman on
your travels, and I have to apologize for detaining you. If
you proceed, let me advise you to visit Niagara about this time.
Take a tour through Canada. After that take your way
through the country generally, not forgetting the caves of Ken-
tucky, and in mid-winter return to Niagara, a splendid sight.
But should you feel inclined to defer your travels, W. E. Burton will be happy to retain your services until the close of the
season."

"What could I do or say?" said Norton, relating the in-
cident. "I literally roared with laughter. He had beaten
me completely. We adjusted the difference, and I remained
with him for two seasons."

on " The **Serious** Family." *Sleek* reads **his**
appeal, and **we** hear a voice saying : " Those
words give comfort to every fainting and
world-worn spirit, good Mr. Aminadab Sleek "
—and **we** know that *Lady Sowerby Creamly*
has spoken, and that Mrs. Hughes is before us.
Of this estimable **lady** and admirable actress,
much more might **be** said than present space
will allow. **Almost as familiar a** figure as the
manager himself, for years **she** enacted those
characters which were peculiarly her fôrte, and
was identified with all the **success** and shared
all the fame of the renowned theatre. We can
recall no instance of her having disappointed
an audience ; **and though, in the** course of her
long service, she may have assumed uncon-
genial parts, yet so intelligent **was** she, so
thorough, so conscientious, that, in spite of un-
suitableness, her performance was always **ac-**
ceptable and meritorious. *Lady Duberly,* in
" The Heir-at-Law," *Mrs. Malaprop,* in " **The**
Rivals," *Lucretia McTab,* in " The Poor **Gen-**
tleman," **were her** accustomed line, and well

indeed she played them. *Widow Warren*, in
" The Road to Ruin," *Mrs. Skewton*, in " Dombey and Son," *Betsy Trotwood*, in " David Cop-
perfied," were kindred felicitous portraitures ;
and no one can think of Burton as *Sleek* and
Toodle without instantly associating Mrs.
Hughes as *Lady Creamly* and *Mrs. Toodle*.
How many times did they play those parts together ! In all those lighter pieces and farces
Burton made so popular and famous, she was
his ally and strong support ; and no history of
the drama of that period can be written without conspicuous mention of her name ; nor can
the professional career and triumphs of Bur-
ton be recounted without suggestion and re-
membrance of Mrs. Hughes. Their professional relation was perfectly harmonious, and
she was with him to the last. She went with
him from Chambers Street to the New The-
atre, and when that was given up accompanied
him on all his starring tours, acting with him
when he appeared for the last time in New
York, and when he acted for the last time in

his life at Hamilton, Canada. In a speech Burton once made, he thus referred to their theatrical relations: "I have been her father, her son, her uncle, her first husband, her second husband, and her third husband, her friend, and her disconsolate widower, and I have liked her better and better in each relation!"

Even as far back as 1826 Mrs. Hughes was a great favorite. H. B. Phelps, in his valuable work known as "Players of a Century," gives a notice of the press she received for a benefit night at.that period, which he says is worth preserving as a model: "Mrs. Hughes takes her benefit at the theatre to-night. It would be an insult to the generous enthusiasm of her numerous admirers, to say another word on the subject."

As it cannot fail to be of interest to readers of this volume, we copy from Mr. Phelps's book a reply to a letter addressed by him to the Hon. Charles Hughes, State Senator, asking information respecting Mrs. Hughes's subsequent history.

" DEAR SIR:—Mrs. Esther Hughes, formerly Mrs.
Young, **was my** mother. She died upon her farm,
three miles from this village (Sandy Hill, N. Y.),
on the 15th of April, 1867, at the age of seventy-
five, from the effects of an accident (falling down
stairs, caused by vertigo). She had left the stage
before the war, her last engagement being a travelling tour with W. E. Burton, in the South and
North. She was acting in Albany as Mrs. Young
when the war of **1812** was declared, and I have
often heard her speak of Solomon Southwick and
of John O. Cole, **who** was a boy in Southwick's
office. Her many years of theatrical life speak for
themselves."

We have heretofore alluded to the Miss
Agnes Roberston of long ago ; and now a mem-
ory steals in upon us of her début at Burton's,
and of her enchanting performance in the pro-
tean play of " The Young Actress." Of the
half dozen parts assumed, the Scotch lassie and
the Irish lad still haunt us. The highland fling
of the one and the " Widow Machree " of the
other were charming **to** see and hear ; and, indeed, Miss Robertson was charming altogether.

We could give a long list of actors and ac-

tresses who from **year to year were enrolled in**
the Chambers Street company, **and whose ef-**
forts are pleasantly remembered. We **do not**
mean to slight them; **but we** must hasten
toward **our** appointed goal. One actress, however, a recognized favorite in New York **long**
before her engagement with Burton, which **ter-**
minated **with her** farewell **to** the stage, deserves
more than a passing notice, **for** the **pleasure**
she gave **was as** pure **and** healthful **as it** was
winsome and bright. **We refer** to Miss Mary
Taylor—"**Our Mary,**"—**better known and es-**
teemed than any actress **of her day,** except
Charlotte Cushman, **that we** can **recall.**

We shall not **dwell** upon **any part of** her
career, **nor** examine her dramatic **capabilities.**
She never appeared without eliciting **the** warmest **of** welcomes; and when **we try to** think of
the many characters we saw her in, we **find our-**
selves remembering only how **sweet and good**
she **was. We** were present **at her** farewell
benefit, and during the speech Mr. Burton made
for her the emotion throughout the house, at

the thought of parting, was as sincere as it was
deep.   She stood, visibly affected, in the midst
of her companions, and when the curtain fell
there was a sigh, as if the audience had lost a
friend.

We have endeavored in the foregoing to in-
dicate the strength of the Chambers Street
company, and we think the reader cannot fail
to be impressed by the exhibit.   The fact of
such dramatic portraiture being easy, seems to
us a striking proof of its supreme excellence.
The majority of them were they living now
might be comedy stars.   When we have Jefferson, Raymond, Fawcett Rowe, Stuart Rob-
son, and Florence, starring about the country,
playing their one part hundreds of nights,
what shall we think of Burton, Placide, Blake,
Brougham, Lester, Johnston, and the rest, appearing together nightly in characters of varied
but equal dramatic power?   There has been a
great change since then.   The name of the
places of amusement now is legion, and one
bright star in the heaven of scenic splendor

consoles the public for the loss of a concentra-
tion of wit and genius. As we recall for a moment all that bright array, we are taken back
through the maze of distance, and old familiar
forms arise ; we see the glimmer of accustomed
footlights; the scene is alive with well-known
faces ; we even hear voices that we know ; we
join in the old-time plaudits—and forget how
many years have rolled between! There is no
retrospection without its tinge of sadness.
" Never to return " is the refrain of human
memory. How beautifully Holmes expresses
it in " The Last Leaf ":

> " The mossy marbles rest
> On the lips that he has pressed,
>   In their bloom ;
> And the names he loved to hear,
> Have been carved for many a year
>   On the tomb."

The years of the Chambers Street Theatre
were fruitful in dramatic events. We have already mentioned " Dombey and Son," in 1848 ;
and that signal triumph was followed by
" David Copperfield," " Oliver Twist," " Nicho-

las Nickleby," and "The Pickwickians." The
immortal *Toodles* was first seen October 2,
1848, and an account of that performance will
be found in our Recollections. It became
later the custom of the management to present
"The Serious Family" and "The Toodles"
every Tuesday and Friday in each week, so
great **was the** popularity of those pieces.
People came from all parts of the country to
see them; parents brought their families and
relatives; and one middle-aged couple, a husband **and** wife, never failed, for successive
seasons, to occupy the same seats at every representation. All the old comedies were given
in due course, **with** that perfection of **cast to**
which we have alluded, and those pieces made
famous **by** Burton's acting—such as "The
Breach of Promise," "Charles XII.," "Happiest **Day** of my Life," "Paul Pry," "Family
Jars," "Soldier's Daughter," "Charles II.,"
"How **to** Make Home Happy," etc., (and
which now seem for ever lost,)—were a con-
stant source of joyous pleasure. The wisdom

MR. LUITON AS TIMOTHY TOODLE.

and good judgment of the manager were conspicuous in the nightly programmes, and it
may here be said that no theatrical caterer
ever excelled Burton in an acute perception
of what was needful to meet the public taste,
and in providing the requisite entertainment.
To wide experience he added intuitive appreciation of stage effect, and his extensive knowledge of the drama was seen in the disciplining
of his forces and in his sagacious distributions.
It must not be forgotten that as manager as
well as actor Burton shone in the prosperity
and fame of his theatre ; and it will not be
when now we touch on the Shakespearian revivals that lent such beauty, grace, and dignity
to his stage, and revealed the manager in the
gracious aspect of a profound and reverent
student of the mighty dramatist. These revivals were the crowning triumphs of Burton's
management. The production of " A Midsummer Night's Dream," " Twelfth Night,"
" The Tempest," " Winter's Tale," " The
Merry Wives of Windsor," marked an era in

theatrical representation, for up to that time
no attempt had been made so ambitious ; and
the success that attended the enterprise was in
all respects richly deserved. " A Midsummer
Night's Dream," in particular, won universal admiration. The fairy portion was so beautiful ;
the play before the duke so capital ; that Shakespeare's creation acted **upon** the public like a
revelation, and heart and mind felt the glow of
a new sensation. The notices of the press were
so unqualified **in** their praise of " A Mid-
summer Night's Dream," that they were
gathered and issued in a pamphlet as a tribute
to the achievement. The effect **of** the succeeding revivals **was** similar in kind, and the
people marvelled at the resources of a manage-
ment that on so limited a stage could produce
such wonderful results. And with these plays
of Shakespeare came the impersonations of
Nick Bottom, Sir Toby Belch, Caliban, Autoly-
***cus*, and** *Falstaff*—never to be forgotten by
those who witnessed them, and of which a
more extended review **is** given in our Recollec-

tions. It only needed Shakespeare to round
the glory of Chambers Street ; after that there
were no more worlds to conquer.

Following the years, we find a record of "As
You Like It," produced for the benefit of the
American Dramatic Fund at the Astor Place
Opera-House, January 8, 1850, in which Burton
appeared as *Touchstone*, with a cast including
Hamblin, Bland, Jordan, Chippendale, Chapman, Miss Cushman, Mrs. Abbott, Mrs. Walcott,
and Mrs. J. Gilbert. In the same year he
played a short engagement at the Chatham
Theatre, and also essayed to revive the old
Olympic, but the division of attraction was of
brief duration. His home was in Chambers
Street, and there, to borrow from Lord Tenny-
son, the banner of Burton blew. The usual even
tenor of the theatre was varied by new accessions to the company, and by first appearances,
and other interesting events. The present
Miss Maggie Mitchell appeared June 2, 1851,
as *Julia*, in "The Soldier's Daughter"; but we
cannot say positively that the occasion was

her stage débût.   May 3, 1852, was the farewell
benefit of Mary Taylor, to which reference has
already been made. September 6th of the
same year was the date of the "Centenary
Festival of the Introduction of the Drama into
America," at Castle Garden, and we find Burton
figuring in the elaborate and attractive programme as *Launcelot Gobbo*, in "The Merchant
of Venice."   Miss Agnes Robertson made her
New York débût October 22, 1853, and November 23d of the same year witnessed the
production of "The Fox Hunt," an original
comedy by Dion Boucicault, in which Burton
appeared as *William Link*.   In 1854, that long
baronet, Sir William Don, entered upon the
scene, and in the same year (December 18th) a
benefit to Morris Barnett occurred, on which
occasion "The Serious Family" was given
with all the honors. Mr. H. A. Perry made
his débût in 1856, playing *Gossamer*, in "Laugh
When You Can," and that actor was also seen
as *Leontes*, in "Winter's Tale."

   Every summer for several years, during the

recess at Chambers Street, Burton played engagements at Niblo's with a selection from his
company, and was seen at that resort in a round
of his favorite characters. This was a great
boon to strangers visiting the city, and to those
whose circumstances kept them in town. It
was some consolation to be moved to mirth,
and there never was any disaffection in Burton's
summer constituency. But the theatrical tide
was setting uptown, and the rapid growth of
the city counselled a removal to more available
neighborhoods ; and so, following the current,
the manager bid farewell to the scene of so
many triumphs, and leased the building origi-
nally known as Tripler Hall, calling it the
Metropolitan, or, as stated by Ireland, "Burton's New Theatre," where he opened September 8, 1856, with " The Rivals."

The Chambers Street Theatre was opened
July 10, 1848, and was closed September 6,
1856. The eight years of its existence are
replete with fascinating dramatic history, and
are a copious and important contribution to

the annals of the stage.   It was the school of
many an actor who rose to fame, and the most
famous actors **of** the time were seen upon its
boards.   It was the birthplace of plays and
characters never excelled in their effect upon
an audience, and its record is graced by a noble
and poetic celebration of Shakespeare's immortal works.   And who shall say how many
hearts were lightened, and spirits cheered, by
the good genius of mirth that presided there?

1856–1860.

It goes without saying that the New Theatre,
to those who had been accustomed to the cosi-
ness of Chambers Street, was not *Burton's.*
The home feeling so peculiar to the other
house **could not** readily be reproduced in the
spacious auditorium of the Metropolitan.   The
far-reaching stage seemed alien and unreal, and
the lofty walls were cold and unfamiliar.   There
were changes in the company, too; old favor-
ites were missing, and a kindred interest was

not awakened by new-comers. **But** the manager was there, and **with** wonted energy began
the campaign. The first season was prosperous,
and many of the well-known Chambers Street
pieces were revived and given with effect.
Daniel Setchell made his appearance September 25, 1856, and grew rapidly in public favor.
This comedian at a later date essayed **the part**
of *Aminadab Sleek ;* but, as Ireland observes,
" Burton's *Sleek* alone filled **the public mind,"**
and the effort was not encouraged. The Irish
comedian, John Collins, was seen about this
time, and in November **Dion** Boucicault **and**
wife opened **an** engagement. January 13,
1857, Burton played *Dogberry* for the first time
in New York, **and the** same year (May 14th)
Edwin Booth appeared at the New Theatre
as *Richard III.* It was in this year (October)
that Burton was seen in Albany for the first
time, playing a round of his famous parts ; and
it is interesting to note that the present Joe
Jefferson, then **at Laura** Keene's, "during the
absence of Burton," to quote Ireland again,

" was recognized as the best low comedian
in town." Burton also appeared in Boston for
the first time in 1857, opening in *Captain
Cuttle*. His reception was so extraordinary in
warmth and enthusiasm that he lost control of
himself and could not speak for several minutes. This engagement was at the Boston
Theatre, and every night the house was
crammed. He visited Boston again in 1858,
and with the same gratifying success.

It is not impossible that these starring tours
suggested to Burton a new and prosperous field
of activity, and perhaps some physical symp-
tom dictated relief from the strain and respon-
sibility of management. From whatever cause,
after another season of varying fortune, the
Metropolitan was given up (1858), and he commenced a starring tour with the highest success, "his name and fame," says Ireland,
" being familiar in every quarter of the Union,
and more surely attractive than any other
theatrical magnet that could be presented."

In conjunction with Mrs, Hughes and a few

members of his former company, he opened an engagement at Niblo's, July 4, 1859, playing to crowded houses. His last appearance in New York was at the same theatre, on the occasion of his benefit, October 15, 1859, playing *Toodle* in the afternoon, and *Mr. Sudden, Toby Tramp,* and *Micawber* in the evening, supported by Mrs. Hughes as *Mrs. Toodle, Mrs. Trapper,* and *Betsy Trotwood.* " On the day and evening of his benefit," says Ireland, " more than six hundred persons who had paid for tickets received their money back from the box-office, not being able to obtain admission."

On Saturday, December 3, 1859, Mr. Burton started for Hamilton, Canada, to fulfil an engagement there and at Toronto. A terrible snow-storm was met on the way ; the train was blocked ; and the delay and discomfort consequent were almost unendurable. While recovering from the exposure and fatigue, Mr. Burton wrote the following letter to his children, and we are kindly permitted to make use of it in this volume. It will be read with interest,

not only for its feeling, but for its graphic
vigor of narration and humorous spirit.   And
we believe it was the **last** letter he ever
wrote.

HAMILTON, CANADA ;
Sunday, December 4, 1859.

My DARLING CHILDREN :

Here I am, in this **provincial** city **of** the West-
ern wilderness, **snowed** up, 500 miles away from
my dear home **and** my precious treasures.   Such
a day and night as **we** had yesterday I hope
never to go through **again.** You remember how
warm it **was** on Friday ? positively hot ; and on
the next morning the weather was cold as New
Year's, but clear and brisk, and the icy tone of the
atmosphere seemed to agree with me.   We reached
Albany in good order, and started at twelve on the
long trip to the Suspension Bridge, over 300 miles,
with **a** light fall of snow, blown about in every direction by **a very** low sort of **a** high wind.   As
we got on our way we found the snow getting
deeper, and the flats of the Mohawk River cov-
ered with ice.   We dined at Utica—a pretty fair
meal, with cold plates and Dutch waiters, who
looked **cold too.** When we changed cars at Roches-
ter the wind blew ferociously, and the snow fell
heavily, so much so that some fears were expressed

that a drift might form on some part of the road
and prevent our progress for a while. At the Suspension Bridge, at half-past twelve **in** the **night, I**
had to get **out of the car** and wade ankle deep in
snow to the open road beside the baggage-car, and
pick out and give checks for our wagon-load of
trunks, seeing them safely deposited in another car
for transportation into Canada. I thought this **was**
a hard job, but **it** was nothing to what I had to do
in Canada, and really a pleasant little episode compared with my doings hereafter. We crossed the
Suspension Bridge within sight of the Falls of
Niagara, but we saw them not. The wind howled
as we passed over that fearful gulf, and drowned
the roaring of the Falls and the rumbling of **the**
rapids as they boiled along some 170 feet below us.
I confess that I rejoiced in reaching *terra firma,*
even on the cold, inhospitable land **of** Canada.
Well, we thought we were snugly housed for the
balance of our journey, **some** forty-four miles to
Hamilton, where we intended to rest for the night
(at two in the morning) and pass a cheerful Canadian
Sunday in our own rooms looking at the snow,
when we **were** roused from our seats : "Change
cars and re-check your baggage." **Out** we turned,
bundles, bags, shawls, top-coat, brandy bottle,
cough mixture, papers, books, and growls, leaving
behind my old travelling cap, which I have had for

years, and is now gone for ever. When I got out I
had to jump into a bed of snow up to my knees,
wade a quarter of a mile through the unbroken
whiteness to a stand of cars inhumanly situated far
from the shelter of the dépôt or the lee of any
building whatever. There, in that snow, without
any feeling in my feet, the wild wind whistling no
end of Verdi overtures with ophicleide accompani-
ment in the snort of various engines, I had to select
my nine packages, see them weighed, have them
checked, wait while the numbers of the checks were
written down, copied off for **me,** and a receipt written for the payment imposed on me for extra baggage. If I had not been so miserably perished
with **cold,** I could have felt some pity for the poor
officials who had to do all this, not only for me, but
for some twenty others, and **in·the** open air too.
But it seemed that I had all **the** baggage in the car.
"Who owns 57,467?" "I do." "Why, you have
baggage enough for a dozen." And it was so. The
nine boxes looked like ninety in **the** confused atmosphere of steam and drifting snow. "That 's
all right, sir." "Then why don't you put the
trunks in the baggage car?" "So we will when
they have passed the customs "!!!!!!!

Yes, **my** darlings, at that hour, past midnight, in
the open snow-storm, with a wind that killed old
Cuttle's "What blew each indiwiddiwal hair from

off yer 'ed," in a blinding drift of frozen crystals
biting each feature and driving their minute but
piercing angles into every pore, I had to wait the
presence and the pleasure of Victoria's excisemen,
to say whether my baggage might or might not pass
duty free into her infernal dominions. I had one
cheerful and pleasant thought that filled my bosom
with religious delight while I waited. I remembered
playing *Harrop* in the drama of " The Innkeeper's
Daughter,"—he is an old smuggler, and *shoots the
exciseman.* I remembered that when I fired the
pistol and the victim dropped, I exclaimed "He 's
done for!" and the audience laughed and applauded!
Yes, the discriminating public applauded me for
killing that exciseman! Oh, was it to do again!
How well I could kill that Canadian gauger here, in
the snow-storm, at midnight, on the banks of the
mad Niagara! Don't be alarmed, darlings. I
did n't kill him. He came at last, booted up to
his middle, with a Canadian capote and hood, and
a leather belt buckled tightly around his waist.
But, despite his Canadian costume, the Cockney
stuck out boldly all over him. He had a roast-
beef-and-porter look, red cheeks, and big English
whiskers. Again I had to go over my list, "great
box, little box, bandbox, bundle," to the potentate
of the tariff. I gave him my honor as a gentleman,
etc., and then told him my profession, and, oh ! my

loves—oh ! my darling children—what is fame ? *he
had never heard of Mr. Burton, the comedian !* Of
course, after that, you agree with me that he ought
to be killed at once, "without remorse or dread."
And he had such an aggravating smell of hot steak
and brandy-and-water. Now, I suppose you think
that my *Ledger* story of intense interest, describing
the agonies of a middle-aged (or more so) individual,
is over. Not a bit of it. The fifth act is to come.
We were jogging along in the cars, slowly crunch-
ing the hard snow on the rails, when we came
gradually to a full stop. Presently whisperings
were heard, occasional and inquisitive male passengers braved even the fury of the storm, and went
abroad to see what was the matter, and in a few
minutes we learned that there was a " break in the
road." You will ask the meaning of the phrase—
so did I, without avail. Gradually the passengers
withdrew from the car (we had but one) and I was
compelled to look for myself. There had been a
collision, or rather an overtaking, for a fast passen-
ger train ran into a freight train, and fearful work
they made of it. I went back for Mrs. Hughes and
the bags, coats, and books. Heaven knows how we
got along, in such a fearful storm, knee-deep in
snow and the track full of holes, with a yawning
gulf on each side. When at last we reached our
place of refuge, we found the car so high off the

rail that it seemed impossible to mount it. Some
gentlemen helped Mrs. Hughes in, with such **exer-**
tions that I expected to see my **dear old** friend
pulled into bits. Then your poor father was left to
his **fate.** I got up—don't ask me how, but when I get
home I 'll climb into my bedroom window from the
street, to show you how I did it. We had **with us**
in the car an admiring friend from Detroit, who
claimed relationship with me because his son married Niblo's niece. Well, we mustered **in the car,**
wet, weary, excited, and chilled to the centre. Oh !
my precious ones, did n't that **brandy bottle** come
in well in that scene ? **How I** let them smell it, and
only smell it ! How I **took** a drink and smacked
my lips, and drank again, and **did** n't **I** win the
heart of old Niblo's brother's daughter's husband's
father by giving him a big drink? At last we
started, slowly, backed into Hamilton **at** half-past
four in the morning, **with** snow two feet deep in the
streets. Half **an** hour's ride in **a** dilapidated article
of the omnibus genus, and we were dumped at a
place **a** cad called **the** "Hanglo-American 'Otel,"
recommended me by Miss Niblo's marital ancestor.
A **fire in** my **room,** a quiet night's rest, a good
breakfast (first-class venison **steak), and I** feel quite
well. **My** feet were wet. My boots could hardly
be pulled off, and in revenge to-day they won't be
pulled **on.** Now am I not a brave old papa to

carry a heart disease **and** a nervous cough through such scenes ?

We are now forty miles from Toronto, whither we proceed at nine in the morning. I hear melancholy doings are prevalent at the place we are bound to, and this deep snow will not make it any better. If business is bad, I shall stay but one week, and **go** to Rochester for the second week.

I am afraid our plants at Glen Cove were badly hurt by the cold spell coming on so suddenly. I hope this weather has **not** increased your coughs. My cough is still troublesome, but **I** am every way better.

May the great God of goodness keep His blessing on **all** my children ; may they keep in health, and in **the** spirit **of** love with each other, is the nightly prayer of

Their affectionate father,

W. E. BURTON.

The last appearance of the comedian on any **stage was at Mechanics'** Hall, Hamilton, Canada, **December** 16, 1859. He played *Aminadab Sleek* and *Goodluck* **in** " John Jones." He returned from the **trip in an** almost exhausted condition, and, after lingering for nearly two months, suffering greatly, died of enlargement

of the heart, February 10, 1860. Mr. Burton
left a wife and three daughters, all of whom
are living. His remains were interred in
Greenwood Cemetery.

The following is a list of parts acted by Mr.
Burton, and though probably there are many
omissions, it fully justifies Ireland's observation
that his repertory was extended almost indefi-
nitely, and " carried into a range, where, if he
was sometimes excelled by Placide and Blake,
his rivalry was such as to demand every effort
on their part to retain their generally acknowl-
edged superiority." It may be mentioned that
the parts of *Aminadab Sleek* and *Timothy
Toodle* were acted by Burton respectively six
hundred and six hundred and forty times.

LIST OF CHARACTERS PERFORMED BY MR. BURTON.

CHARACTERS.	PLAYS.
HOST, FALSTAFF,	in " The Merry Wives of Windsor."
DROMIO,	in " The Comedy of Errors."
DR. OLLAPOD, SIR ROBERT BRAMBLE,	in " The Poor Gentleman."
MUNNS,	in " Forty Winks."

CHARACTERS.		PLAYS.
JOB THORNBERRY,	**in**	" John Bull."
LAUNCELOT GOBBO,	in	" The Merchant of Venice."
HARROP,	in	" The Innkeeper's Daughter."
BOTTOM,	in	" A Midsummer Night's Dream.**"**
CALIBAN,	in	" The Tempest."
SIR TOBY BELCH,	in	" Twelfth Night."
CAPT. CUTTLE,	in	" Dombey and Son."
TIMOTHY TOODLE,	in	" The Toodles."
AMINADAB SLEEK,	**in**	" The Serious Family."
VAN DUNDER,	in	" The Dutch Governor."
TRIPLET,	**in** "	Masks and Faces."
BOB ACRES,	**in** "	The Rivals."
DR. PANGLOSS, LORD DUBERLY,	in	" The Heir-at-Law.**"**
BILLY LACKADAY,	in	" Sweethearts and Wives."
PILLICODDY,	in	" Poor Pillicoddy."
TOBY TRAMP,	in	" The Mummy."
TONY LUMPKIN.	in	" She Stoops to Conquer."
CHAS. GOLDFINCH,	in	" The Road to Ruin."
JACQUES STROP,	in	" Robert Macaire."
SEPTIMUS PODDLE,	**in**	" Take That Girl Away."
JEM BAGGS,	**in**	" The Wandering Minstrel."
SLASHER,	**in**	" Slasher and Crasher."
JOHN UNIT,	in	" Self."
GREGORY THIMBERWELL,	in	"State Secrets."
BONNYCASTLE,	in	" The Two Bonnycastles."
JEREMIAH CLIP,	**in**	" The Widow's Victim."
DIMPLE,	**in**	" Leap Year."
MEGRIM,	in	" Blue Devils."
FELIX FUMER,	in	" The Laughing Hyena."
LA FLEUR,	**in**	" Animal Magnetism."
TOM RIPSTONE,	**in**	" Evil Genius."

CHARACTERS.	PLAYS.
TOM NODDY,	in " Tom Noddy's Secret."
SNOBBINGTON,	in " A **Good** Night's Rest."
PETTIBONE,	in " A Kiss in the Dark."
PAUL PRY,	in " Paul Pry."
JOE **BAGS**,	in " **Wanted** 1000 Milliners."
SIR **OLIVER SURFACE**, SIR **PETER TEAZLE**,	} in " **The School for Scandal**."
MEDDLE,	in " **London** Assurance."
THOMAS **TROT**,	in " **Paris** and London."
WORMWOOD,	in " **The Lottery** Ticket."
WADDILOVE,	in " **To** Parents and Guardians."
SQUEERS,	in " **Nicholas** Nickleby."
MICAWBER,	in " David Copperfield."
JOHN MILDMAY,	in " Still Waters Run Deep."
SUDDEN,	in " The Breach of Promise."
CALEB QUOTEM,	in " The Review."
PEDRO,	in " Cinderella."
SCHNAPPS,	in " **The Naiad** Queen."
MR. BUMBLE,	in " **Oliver Twist**."
PETER SPYK,	in " The Loan of a Lover."
MOCK DUKE,	in " The Honeymoon."
SIR WM. FONDLOVE,	in " The Love **Chase.**"
CODDLE, DOVE,	} in " Married **Life.**"
DOMINIE SAMPSON,	in " Guy Mannering."
PETER,	in " The Stranger."
MR. GILMAN,	in " Happiest Day **of** My Life."
GRAVES,	in " Money."
DUKE'S SERVANT,	in " High Life Below Stairs."
SAM WELLER,	in " Pickwick."
DON WHISKERANDOS,	in " The Critic."
SIMPSON,	in " **Simpson &** Co."

CHARACTERS.	PLAYS.
TOUCHSTONE,	in " As You Like It."
TOM TAPE,	in " Sketches in India."
TONY BAVARD,	in " The French Spy."
SCRUB,	in " Now-a-Days."
BROWN,	in " Kill or Cure."
FLUID,	in " The Water Party."
NICHOLAS RUE,	in " Secrets Worth Knowing."
MR. FLARE,	in " Such As It Is."
FREDERICK STORK,	in " The Prince's Frolic."
MR. TWEEDLE,	in " The Broken Heart."
GALOCHARD,	in " The King's Gardener."
SNOWBALL,	in " The Catspaw."
WAGGLES,	in " Friend Waggles."
EUCLID FACILE,	in " Twice Killed."
JENKINS,	in " Gretna Green."
BULLFROG,	in " The Rent Day."
BOX,	in " Box and Cox."
MRS. MACBETH,	in " Macbeth Travestie."
CHRISTOPHER STRAP,	in " Pleasant Neighbors."
OLD RAPID,	in " A Cure For the Heartache."
COL. DAMAS,	in " The Lady of Lyons."
VERGES, DOGBERRY,	in " Much Ado About Nothing."
JOHN SMITH,	in " Nature's Nobleman."
EPHRAIM JENKINSON,	in " The Vicar of Wakefield."
MICHAEL,	in " Love in Humble Life."
TETTERBY,	in " The Haunted Man."
MR. MENNY,	in " Socialism."
PIERRE DE LA ROCHE,	in " The Midnight Watch."
SPHINX,	in " The Sphinx."
TOM BOBOLINK,	in " Temptation."
PICADILLY,	in " Burton's New York Directory."

CHARACTERS.	PLAYS.
JUSTICE WOODCOCK,	in " Love in a Village."
BILL,	in " Peep From the Parlor Windows."
HARESFOOT,	in " Life Among the Players."
NOGGS,	in " The Mormons."
MARC ANTONY BAROWN,	in " A Great Tragic Revival."
SIGNOR TOPAZ,	in " Fascination."
VANDAM,	in " Wall Street."
COL. ROCKET,	in " Old Heads and Young Hearts."
VON FIEZENSPAN,	in " The Slave Actress."
JONAS BLOT,	in " The Poor Scholar."
EPAMINONDAS,	in " Genevieve."
ANTHONY GAB,	in " The Witch Wife."
BONUS,	in " Laugh When You Can."
WILLIAM RUFUS,	in " Helping Hands."
COL. GOLDIE,	in " 'T is Ill Playing with Edged Tools."
BERRYMAN,	in " False Pretences."
DICK,	in " Ellen Wareham."
SUCKLING,	in " Education."
SPATTERDASH,	in " The Young Quaker."
BOB CLOVER,	in " Married an Actress."
OLD REVEL,	in " School for Grown Children."
GILES GRIZZLE,	in " Stag Hall."
BALTHAZAR,	in " Player's Plot."
WILLIAM LINK,	in " The Fox-Hunt."
BLANQUET,	in " The Lancers."
BRAINWORM,	in " Every Man in His Humor."
MANUEL COGGS,	in " Married by Force."
RATTAN,	in " The Beehive."
GREGORY GRIZZLE,	in " My Wife and Umbrella."
DELPH,	in " Family Jars."
TEWBERRY,	in " A Heart of Gold."
JUPITER,	in " Apollo in New York."

CHARACTERS.	PLAYS.
COUNT VENTOSO,	in " Pride Must Have a Fall."
DR. LACQUER,	in " Our Set."
DE BONHOMME,	in " A Nice Young Man."
SIR HIPPINGTON MIFF,	in "Comfortable Lodgings."
MAXIMUS HOGSFLESH,	in " Barbers at Court."
FRIGHT,	in "Crimson Crimes."
INFANTE FURIBOND,	in " Invisible Prince."
MR. GREENFINCH,	in "Duel in the Dark."
TIMOTHY QUAINT,	in "Soldier's Daughter."
SIR SIMON SLACK,	in "Spring and Autumn."
PEEPING TOM,	in " All at Coventry."
TRISTAM SAPPY,	in " Deaf as a Post."
CODGER,	in "You 're Another."
TACTIC,	in " My Fellow Clerk."
TONY NETTLETOP,	in " Love in a Maze."
TOBIAS SHORTCUT,	in " The Spitfire."
BOB TICKET,	in "An Alarming Sacrifice."
JEREMY DIDDLER,	in " Raising the Wind."
JACK HUMPHREYS,	in " Turning the Tables."
MAW-WORM,	in " The Hypocrite."
DAFFODIL TWOD,	in " The Ladies' Man."
GOLIGHTLY,	in " Lend Me Five Shillings."
CHRISTOPHER CROOKPATH,	in " Upper Ten and Lower Twenty."
GHOST,	in " Hamlet Travestie."
DIGGORY,	in " The Spectre Bridegroom."
BENJAMIN BUZZARD,	in " The Two Buzzards."
MARMADUKE MOUSER,	in "Betsey Baker."
CRACK,	in " The Turnpike Gate."
BILLY BLACK,	in " 100-Pound Note."
CAPT. COPP,	in " Charles the Second."
MARALL,	in " New Way to Pay Old Debts."

CHARACTERS.	PLAYS.

TOBIAS SHORTCUT, **in** " The Cockney."

PETER POPPLES, **in " Man of** Many Friends."

ADAM BROCK, in "Charles the Twelfth."

RICHARD **PRIDE,** in " Janet Pride."

POLONIUS, ⎫
FIRST GRAVE-DIGGER, ⎬ in " Hamlet."

FIRST WITCH, in " Macbeth."

SIR GEORGE THUNDER, **in** " Wild Oats."

GUY GOODLUCK, **in "** John Jones."

MARPLOT, **in** " The Busybody."

JOE SEDLEY, **in "** Vanity Fair."

GIL, in " Giralda."

QUEEN BEE, in **" St. Cupid."**

DABCHICK, in **" How** to Make Home Happy."

SHADOWLY SOFTHEAD, in **"** Not So Bad As We Seem."

SMYTH, in " Mind Your Own Business."

SIR TIMOTHY STILTON, **in** " Patrician and Parvenu."

CARDINAL MAZARIN, in "Youthful Days of Louis XIV."

TWINKS, in **" Mrs. Bunbury's Spoons."**

RECOLLECTIONS

OF

MR. BURTON'S PERFORMANCES

" *And now what rests* **but that we spend** *the time*
With stately triumphs, mirthful **comic** *shows.*"
—SHAKESPEARE.

◆

RECOLLECTIONS.

WHEN **Burton** opened **in** Chambers Street, he was forty-four years old, **in the prime of** life, his powers mature and approaching culmination. Let us endeavor to give a portrait **of** the comedian as he appeared at this time. Above the medium height; rotund in form, yet not cumbersome; limbs well proportioned; deep-chested, with harmonious breadth **of** shoulder; neck short and robust; large and well-balanced head; the hair worn short behind, longer in front, and brushed smartly toward the temples; face clean-shaven; complexion bordering on the florid; full chin and cheeks; eyes seemingly blue or gray, beneath brows not over heavy, and capable of every conceivable expression; nose straight, **and** somewhat sharply inclined; mouth large, the

lips **thin, and** wearing **in repose a** smile half
playful, **half** trenchant.   Such is the picture
memory draws, **the** likeness in some degree
confirmed by engravings in **our** possession.
Outlined thus, and in his **proper** person, he
seemed in **general** aspect **to** blend the suave
respectability of **a bank** president with the
easy-going air **of an** English country squire.
We shall **have** occasion to refer in due course
to the marvellous changes that were possible
to that face and form, when the man became
the actor **and walked** the stage with Momus,
with Dickens, and with Shakespeare.   Promi-
nent among his physical attributes was a clear,
strong voice, capable of a great variety of **in-**
tonations, **and his** delivery was such that no
words of his were **ever** lost in any part of **the
house.**

Before entering the wide field of our memories, we wish to offer some observations respecting the comedian's mental equipment,
and to consider briefly the features of his un-
rivalled powers.   **We have** no doubt but that

the classical education of his youth had much
to do with his early preference for the tragic
muse. His mind, imbued with admiration for
classic form and color, was fed with divine
images, which, while replete with grace and
beauty, bore still the impress of Greek austerity.
He inclined naturally, therefore, toward the
conception of that which was the predominat-
ing influence **in his mental** training. At the
same time, after eschewing his predilections
for tragedy, he found that the classic discipline
had created a receptivity of mind in the highest degree important to his future study ; and
that quickened apprehension proved of inesti-
mable value in his subsequent introduction to
Shakespeare, the old dramatists, and in all his
intellectual excursions.

Yielding to him, then, this vantage-ground
of culture, let us glance at the attributes of his
genius, which entitle him, as we think, to the
claim made for him—namely, one of the greatest actors in his line the stage has known. We
need not specify that line further than to say

that it passes with the title of "low comedy";
but Burton's versatility was so extraordinary,
his repertory so extended, his conceptions so
forcible, that the theatric nomenclature seems
insufficient to define and measure the scope
and range of his abilities. His impersonations,
especially those Shakespearian, were often of
too high an order to be classed under the ac-
cepted notion of low comedy. Let us style
him an expounder and representative of the
Humor of the Drama in all its aspects,
and we shall come nearer to what he really
was. For an all-embracing perception of
humor revealed itself perpetually in his acting.
As the imagination of Longfellow transformed
to organ pipes the musketry of the Springfield
Arsenal, so would Burton change dull inanities
into vital and joyous images. This informing
power, this native faculty of rising superior to
the part assumed, and investing it with un-
dreamed-of humorous interest, was an instinct
of his genius, and gave to all his embodiments
an originality and a flavor peculiarly his own.

The character **mattered** not. It might **be**
Nick Bottom or *Paul Pry*, *Cuttle* or *Micawber*,
Doctor *Ollapod* or *Charles Goldfinch*, *Sleek* or
Toodle. There was the complete identification,
the superlative realization of the author's
meaning ; but the felicitous interpretation, the
by-play, the way of saying **a** thing, the facial
expression—his own and no other man's,—the
Burtonian touch and treatment. In the extravagance of farcical abandon no one **ever** was
funny **as** he. In comic portraits like *Toby
Tramp* or *Jem Baggs*, he absolutely exhaled
mirth ; and we cannot help thinking how perfectly Hazlitt describes him in writing of Liston : " His farce is not caricature ; his drollery
oozes out of his features, and trickles down his
face ; his voice **is a** pitch-pipe **for** laughter."
" We have seen Burton," says Wemyss, " keep
an audience **in roars** of inextinguishable laughter, for minutes in succession, while an expression of ludicrous bewilderment, of blank
confusion, or pompous inflation, settled **upon**
his countenance." And this was penned by

Wemyss **at a time** when *Cuttle, Micawber, Sleek,* and *Toodle* were yet to be.

In thus indicating Burton's natural gifts, we must not lose sight of the study and knowledge necessary to their development and to the achievement of his fame. Let **it** not be supposed that his famous delineations were so many intuitions, easily shaped and clothed by **him** into substantial dramatic form. Easy, in-**deed,** they **might appear in the** handling—**for it** was characteristic of the great comedian **never to seem to** entirely expend himself,—he **always suggested a** reserved force;—but this facile rendering was attained at the expense of **as** much intellectual attrition **as Moore de-clared the melodious** numbers of **his** verse often cost him.

The late Dr. John W. Francis relates a con-versation with the famous George Frederick Cooke, respecting the actor's impersonation of *Sir Pertinax Macsycophant,* and in reply to the question, how he acquired so profound a knowledge of **the** Scotch accentuation, Cooke said: "I studied more than two and a half years in my own room, with repeated intercourse with Scotch society, in order to master the Scottish dialect, before I ventured to appear on the boards in Edinburgh, as *Sir Pertinax*, and when I did, Sawney took me for a native. It was the hardest task I ever undertook." How do we know how many years of thoughtful application the comedian's masterpieces expressed?

Mr. Burton was a student and man of the world as well as actor, and the supremacy of his performances was due to his close and comprehensive study of his author, his acquaintance with dramatic composition, his artistic sense, his thorough knowledge of the stage, his varied experience, his human insight,—the rest, like Dogberry's reading and writing, came by nature.

It is a habit with old play-goers, when over their cakes and ale, to recall the "palmy days" of the drama, and to say: "Ah, you should have seen —— ; he was a great artist—none equal to him nowadays. **Ah,** the stage **has** declined **since** the old time." We do not wholly believe in the drama's decadence, but **as** we enter upon our Recollections we feel that *there* were our palmy days, and the years seem long between. Twenty-four have passed since the comedian died, and there has been no sign of a successor to the mask and mantle. **And it may be** twice—nay, thrice twenty **before the actor shall arise** who will compel us to recall the triumphs of Burton for the sake of comparison.

MR. BURTON IN FARCE.

A man like Mr. Burton, endowed **with keen** humorous perception **and** the mimetic faculty, competent to express easily and with unction every **phase** of mirthful extravagance suggested **by** fancy **and flow of** spirit, must occasionally yield **to the** imperious demands of his nature, and, perforce, when so pressed, he opens the safety-valve of play and gives escape **to his** excess of humor.

In this connection, we are reminded of Sydney Smith, as an example of humorous irrepressibility. Restraint seldom fettered the expression of the witty suggestions of his fancy. It was as natural in him to be gay and mirthful as it was to breathe. His humor welled from a perpetual spring. It was like the profanity of the Scotchman who did n't swear at any thing particular, but just stood in the middle of the road and "swore at large." There is a story that the divine, arriving first at a gathering of notables, was ushered into the drawing-room, which was hung with mirrors on all sides. Seeing himself reflected at all points, he looked around and observed: "Ah, a very respectable collection of clergymen!" Now his only auditor was the servant; but the thought came and was at once expressed. Of course, Sydney Smith could be serious when he wished, as all know who are familiar with his life and works; but he had his play-ground at Holland House and in kindred coteries, where his buoyant spirit worked its own sweet will.

When the clergyman of lugubrious aspect called upon poor Tom Hood, the story goes that the humorist could not help remarking: " My dear Sir, I 'm afraid your religion does n't agree with you ! "—and **we** are quite willing to believe the story to be one of " Hood's Own," for it has all the flavor of the author who gave us "Laughter from Year **to** Year." Instances might be multiplied of this humorous self-abandonment; **but we are** growing digressive. The train of reflection, however, leads us **to** the belief that **Burton's** merry-making powers needed occasionally an avenue of escape ; and the safety-valve, in his case, was often found in **the** farces his acting made so popular—those exhibitions of **fun and** drollery in which, through the lens of memory, we now intend **to view him.**

The farce, by the way, is a thing of the past.   It may almost be said that as a form of the acting drama, at least in America, it has been passed to the limbo of disuse.   Rarely, if **ever,** do our programmes nowadays bear the old, familiar formula : " To conclude with the laughable Farce of ———." We are no longer invited to laugh at the droll situations and funny dialogues contained in the many pieces of Buckstone, Mathews, and Morton ; yet all will admit their efficacy to beguile a lagging hour, and to smooth away the obtrusive wrinkle from the proverbial brow of care. Such, certainly, was the power they exerted in other days ; and perhaps it is to be lamented that the frolic atmosphere diffused by those comic productions is ours no more to make merry and revel in. "Custom exacts, and who denies her sway?" remarks Colman, the younger ; and for many years the design of our managers, in catering for the public, has comprehended the representation of one play only for the performance of an evening ; setting it elaborately, bestowing upon it a wealth of scenic embellishment, and presenting it generally with a due regard to strength and fitness of cast. Many of the standard comedies have been thus illustrated—notably " The

School for Scandal" and "She Stoops to Conquer"; the comedies of Robertson—"Home,"
"Caste," "School," "Ours,"—have been so
rendered at Wallack's, and at the same theatre
that play of charming improbabilities, "Rose-
dale," has enjoyed a periodic return. "Led
Astray," acted so long at the Union Square
Theatre; Mr. Daly's many successful adapta-
tions, and the Irish dramas of Mr. Boucicault;
"The Two Orphans"; "The Banker's Daughter"; "Hazel Kirke";—all these, and more,
are like examples. Mr. Jefferson's "Rip Van
Winkle" suffices for an evening; so also does
Mr. Raymond's *Col. Sellers*, and so also did Mr.
Sothern's *Dundreary*. This new departure
may be a very good departure, for it gives
us perfection in the details of scenery and
costume, and concentrates the managerial
resources in one splendid whole; and we may
add, that a theatrical system is to be com-
mended when it permits the audience to get
comfortably home and to bed before midnight.
But, all the same, if Burton were living and

acting, the farce would hold its own ; and
every auditor would remain to the fall of the
curtain, for the last glimpse of that face, the
last word and action of that comedian who held
such sway over the risibilities of mankind.

If among our readers there should be any
old play-goers, they cannot fail to remember
how often they dropped in for an hour's hilar-
ity with " The Wandering Minstrel," or " Poor
Pillicoddy." For, as previously stated, it was
a circumstance by no means unusual to see
fresh arrivals lining the walls of the theatre,
drawn thither by the potent magnet of Burton
in the farce. It was a matter of almost as
much consequence to know what afterpiece
was on the bill as what comedy. Often, indeed, the effect produced by Burton in some
exceptionally droll part had become so widely
known, that to see him in it was the prime
object of a visit to the theatre ; and if to
the question — " What does Burton play
to-night?" the answer named *Toby Tramp,
Madame* Vanderpants, or the like, it was

enough : " Let us go ! " was the eager excla-
mation.

What a piece of fun was *Toby Tramp*, in
" The Mummy " ! How many who are living
now will laugh as they recall the appearance of
Burton in that close-fitting garment, covered
with hieroglyphics ! The plot is simple and
easily told. *Toby* is an itinerant player, needy
and shabby, out at elbow and out of money ;
and agrees for a cash consideration to personate
a mummy, already sold and promised to an old
antiquarian. As we think of the scene in
which the bargain is concluded we remember
how full of stage strut and quotation Burton
was, and how he embraced the opportunity to
present a specimen of *Toby's* histrionic quality,
selecting the familiar soliloquy of *Richard*, and
giving it as he (*Toby*) declared Shakespeare
ought always to be interpreted. He commenced :

" Now is the winter of our discontent "—

and with the words turned up his coat-collar,

blew his fingers, shivered, and was frozen generally.   Continuing then :

" Made glorious summer by **this sun of York** "—

he instantly **thawed, threw** open **his coat,** puffed, **and from his brow wiped the** perspiration.   And **so he went through the** whole.   At the **words " Grim-visag'd war,"** a gloomy **and** malignant frown darkened **his** features, **which** changed, **as he pronounced "** hath **smooth'd** his **wrinkled front," to a bland** expression **of** peace ;—and **the climax was reached when at** the **lines :**

" He capers nimbly in a lady's chamber,
  To the lascivious pleasing of a lute "—

he executed a fantastic dance, thrumming **the** while an imaginary guitar.

This burlesque, **for** aught **we** know, may have been an interpolation, a contribution of Burton himself to the fund of merriment—one of the instances, in fact, where he dropped the rein and let Momus have his way.   But however **it** came, the travesty created unbounded amusement, and put the audience in the best possible humor; yet we feel how pointless is our sketch to even suggest the facial power, the comic attitudes, the air, the touches of drollery, born of the whole scene; and our readers must summon their imagination to help our failure.

The next scene is the antiquarian's museum, and the mummy is brought in. After the necessary raptures consequent upon such a unique possession, the professor withdraws and the stage is left alone. There lies the mummy in his case, and a pause succeeds. The intent audience observe a slight movement in the box. Slowly the head of Burton is raised, and he glances warily around the room. Raising himself to a sitting posture in the case, he turns toward the audience his marvellous face, on which rests an expression of doleful humiliation. We shall never forget how, finally, he rose to his feet, stepped out of the case, walked abjectly to the foot-lights, looked his disguise all over with intense concern, and then turned to the house—by this time scarcely able to contain itself—and said, with the accent of self-reproach and mortification—" I 'm —— if I 'm not ashamed of myself ! "

Situations follow, affording full opportunity for the display of Burton's humorous characteristics ; but we **need** not pursue them in detail. He frightens everybody **as a** mummy ; makes **love** as a mummy ; **devours** the antiquarian's dinner ; has **his** tragic bursts ;—in **short,** leaves nothing **to be** desired on the part **of those who paid their** money to laugh and be **jolly with him.**

Mad. Vanderpants **was** another uproarious creation, more laughable even, in some ways, than " The Mummy." *Joe Baggs* (Burton) is a lawyer's clerk, and during the absence of his employer on a journey, arranges a programme of deviltry for himself and comrade (T. B. Johnston). *Baggs* becomes *Mad. Vanderpants,* and his companion *Miss Smithers,* her assistant, and they advertise for " A Thousand Milliners." Burton's " make-up " was one of the most astonishing things **we** ever saw, and

Johnston's was by no **means** lacking in artistic
finish.   The milliners arrive (that is a representation), and then ensues an hour of unparal-
leled fun and frolic.   The manner of Burton in
sustaining the character and in replying with
complacent air to the numerous questions
asked **by** the deluded damsels, was so supreme-
ly ludicrous that we pause in writing to laugh
at the remembrance.   Some work is wanted,
and the window shades are unceremoniously
torn down and given to the milliners.   " What
shall we do **with it** ? ask they.   " Do ?" replied
Burton, with imperturbable gravity, " Why,
you can hemstitch it up one side, and back-
stitch it down the other—and then gusset it all
around !"   **The** fun **waxes** fast **and** furious,
when suddenly the employer returns.   The
dénouement can be imagined ; we cannot describe it ;—**but** those **who** remember Burton's
mimetic power, and his faculty to express
abject terror and kindred emotions, can well
understand what a scene of indescribable riotous
humor it was.   And we cannot omit, in refer-

ring to this farce, to mention the admirable support given by the lamented Mrs. Hughes, who, as one of the milliners, contributed largely to the general success by her conscientious acting.

How can we, in this allotted space, deal justly with our crowding memories? What shall we say of *Jem Baggs*, in "The Wandering Minstrel"?—that minstrel whose entrance on the stage was heralded by a sounding strain certainly never before heard on sea or land, and whose appearance, as he emerged from the wing, continuing still the dirge-like air, was a signal for a gleeful burst all over the house. How paint his introduction, under a mistaken identity, into musical society; the situation that follows; his song of "All Around My Hat"; the comic incidents that strew the too-fleeting hour of his career?

How view him as *Pillicoddy*, awaiting with supreme anguish the "turning up" of his wife's "first," through all the phases of ludicrous bravado and comic despair?

How depict him in " Turning the Tables " ? or in " The Siamese Twins "? or in " That Blessed Baby " ? How see him as *Mr. Dabchick*, in " The Happiest Day of My Life " ? or as *Megrim*, in " Blue Devils," and ever so many more ?

And yet we ought to linger on each one ; for we have never seen them since, and it may be we may never see them again—certain is it that we shall never see them so performed. And only for the sake of refreshing a memory of something greater would we wish to behold them now.

In concluding this imperfect tracing of recollection, we are conscious of many deficiencies ; one of these a few final words may supply.

We have said nothing of the individualization of Burton's many characters in farce. It is true that the native hue and flavor of the comedian's humor were so strong, and his physique so pronounced, that he himself was always more or less apparent in whatever guise ; but it would be a great mistake to suppose that in the parts above named there was no essential difference, with respect to portraiture. There **was a** difference, **and it** was clearly marked. Each was **a** picture **by** itself —each a **distinct** characterization ; and in the development **the** author was often left **so** far behind **that the** actor **became** the creator. But **this** loyalty to ideal perception denotes, **as it** seem to us, that even in farcical **abandon** his delineations were shaped and governed by his artistic sense.

MR. BURTON **IN** PARTS HE **MADE** SPECIALLY FAMOUS.

The familiar picture of John Philip Kemble in the character of *Hamlet*, standing at *Ophelia's* grave, in sad retrospection over the skull of Yorick, always impressed us as a revelation of **the** fact that an actor's fame is bequeathed to posterity in the traditions of effect produced by a few celebrated embodiments, and is forever associated with those special triumphs.

That Kemble was a supreme representative of
the impressive school, that he merited the
glowing eulogium contained in Campbell's eloquent verses, there will be no question; but
when we think of him or read of him, the
figure of the Dane looms up in sombre majesty, and we are haunted by the avenging
spirit of Elsinore.

The picture of Edmund **Kean**, as *Richard*,
kneeling at the feet of *Lady Anne*, with the
words, " Take up the sword again, or take up
me," upon his lips, impresses us in the same
way; and any thought of that great tragedian
conjures an attendant vision of the dark and
aspiring *Gloster*.

When, in the years to come, the name of
Jefferson is spoken, will not imagination linger
on *Rip Van Winkle's* long slumber amid the
everlasting hills? and will not Sothern and
Raymond appeal to a future generation as
Dundreary of the glaring eye, and *Sellers* of
the uplifted arm? And we have no doubt
that Mr. Burton is, in the memory of those

now living who saw him, and will be to those who shall know him from tradition and dramatic annals, the actor who was so inimitable as *Captain Cuttle, Aminadab Sleek,* and *Timothy Toodles.* And no wonder. The mere mention of them opens the flood-gate of recollection, and we seem to hear far down the aisles of time the free, glad laughter of delighted audiences. If, haply, in our memories hitherto we have struck in some heart the chord of reminiscence, surely now we may hope to prolong the strain. For, among the many who are still here to tell of their nights at Burton's, few, perchance, will revert to *Bob Acres* or *Goldfinch, Nick Bottom* or *Autolycus;* while all, at the comedian's name, will at once summon the images of *Cuttle, Sleek,* and *Toodles.*

In view of the extraordinary popularity of these performances, we shall treat now of certain parts made specially famous by Mr. Burton, and present in another group a view of other and various characters in his comedy repertory.

A favorite part, and one which always delighted us, was that prince of stage busybodies,
Paul Pry.   The character as Poole drew it affords unusual scope for the exhibition of comic
power, and in Burton's hands its humorous
possibilities were made the most of.   The play
was frequently on the bills, and always drew a
house that followed the comedian through all
his mirth-moving entanglements in a state of
hilarious enjoyment.   The more we think of it,
the more we are disposed to class *Paul Pry* as
one of Burton's masterpieces, so rich was it in
certain phases of humor and so replete with
droll suggestiveness.   It may not, perhaps, be
generally known that Mr. Burton was the second comedian who played the part in England,
and it was a favorite of the renowned Liston,
whose impersonation of it won him fame
and fortune.   There is a story to the effect
that at the last rehearsal of the comedy, previous to its presentation at the Haymarket,
Liston was undecided as to his costume ; and
while on the stage, still doubtful and uncertain,

a workman entered on some errand, wearing a large pair of Cossack trousers, which, it being a wet day, he had tucked into his wellingtons. The appearance of the trousers struck Liston, who adopted the idea; and hence the origin of the dress peculiar to *Pry.* We remember very well the general effect of Burton's " make-up "; can recall various details ; but the point of the trousers is not clear ; so a better memory than ours must determine whether or no Liston's notion was perpetuated by his successor.

We see Burton now, as he entered upon the scene at *Doubledot's* inn with : " Ha ! how d' ye do, Doubledot ? " and we hear him asking with ingratiating audacity question after question, pausing for an answer after each one, and in no wise put out at getting none,—" never miss any thing for the want of asking, you know." Then his lingering departure, and *Doubledot's* fervent : " I 've got rid of him at last, thank heaven ! " No, he returns. " I dropped one of my gloves " (looking about). *Doubledot* waxes impatient and speaks his mind.

" **Mr.** Doubledot," **said** Burton, swelling with
insulted dignity, " I want my property; I want
my property, sir.   When I came in here I had
two gloves, and now—ah—that 's very odd;
I 've got it in my hand all this time ! " (hasty
exit). How little it seems in the telling. The
air of anxiety **on** returning, and the eye-glass
brought into play; the look of injured inno-
cence, the indignant assertion, and then the
sudden collapse—cannot be reproduced in
words.

The piece is full of diverting situations, **but
nothing was more** natural than that Burton
should improve on and **add to** them.   His
bright instinct kindled **the** dry fagots of a
scene till they fairly crackled with merriment.
Certain " business," humorous amplification
of dialogue, a diffusion of comic incident, that
we vividly recall, are not to be found in the
printed " Paul Pry "; and the conclusion **of
the** second **act,** especially, where **the** pistols
are used with such ·ludicrous effect, all that
was Burton's own.   The pistols lay on the

table, left there by *Col. Hardy*, and *Pry* is
alone.   Burton took them up, one in each
hand.   He regarded the weapons fixedly.
Then, with solemn enunciation : " I never
fought a duel ; but if I was called out," ex-
tending an arm, " I say if I was called out "—
bang ! went one of the pistols, and down
dropped Burton, the picture of fright, when
bang ! went the other, and the curtain fell on
the comedian sitting in abject terror, a smok-
ing pistol in each hand, gazing in every direction
for succor, and wildly ejaculating " Murder ! "
Then, at the close of the play, when *Pry* reminds *Col. Hardy* that, thanks to him (*Pry*),
things, after all, have resulted to the satisfaction of everybody, the *Colonel* relaxes his
sternness somewhat and says : " Well, I will
tolerate you ; you shall dine with me to-day."
" Colonel," replied Burton, with airy condescen-
sion, " I 'll dine with you every day."

It was a rare pleasure to see Placide and
Burton in their respective parts ; and as once
again we think of them the Chambers Street

stage is before us, and the garden scene; and
we see *Col. Hardy* place the ladder against the
wall, mount it and peer cautiously over, and
then hastily descend, saying: "I have him;
there he is, crouching on the ground with his
eye at the key-hole"; see him quietly approach
the gate, suddenly open it, and once again as of
old, Burton tumbles in, umbrella and all, with
" How are you, Colonel! I 've just dropped in!"

He will never more drop in for us, nor does
it seem likely that in our day another *Paul Pry*
will appear. The play may have been performed in New York since the comedian's
death, and we seem dimly to remember that it
was; but we have no recollection beyond the
simple circumstance. We feel sure, however,
that public interest in it ceased with the departure of its last great representative; and
equally sure that in the memory of those who
saw it, Burton's *Paul Pry* remains a famous
creation of delightful humor.

What shall we say of *Captain Cuttle?* How
many readers and lovers **of** Dickens thronged

the theatre in the old days to witness that wonderful reproduction ? and how many to whom Dickens was but a name were led by the impersonation to study the pages of the great novelist ? It is certain that Burton by his sympathetic and admirable portrayal awakened a fresh interest in the enchanting story, so potent to excite intellectual pursuit is fine and sagacious interpretation. " Dombey and Son " was one of the great triumphs of the Chambers Street Theatre, and not to have seen it consti-tuted an offence against public sentiment utterly without palliation. That it was Charles Dickens dramatized by John Brougham was enough of itself to claim respectful attention : and when Burton added the crowning effect of his acting of *Cuttle*, then indeed was the dramatic feast complete. Nothing could be clearer than that the comedian had made care-ful and conscientious study of his author, and nothing surer than that the portrait was con-ceived in an appreciative and loving spirit. If those familiar with the character as depicted

by Dickens discerned at times certain felicitous
touches in Burton's delineation which suggested an originality of method and treatment,
the points were due, we think, to the genius of
the novelist acting upon the actor's imagination, and kindling it to the expression of cog-
nate verisimilitude.

What a memory it is to linger on ! How
the form comes back, clad in the white suit ;
the high collar, like a small sail, and the black
silk handkerchief with flaring ends loosely
encircling it ; the head bald at top, a shining
pathway between the bristling hair on each
side; the bushy eyebrows arching the reveren-
tial eyes ; the knob-environed nose ; the waist-
coat with buttons innumerable ; the glazed
hat under his left arm ; the hook gravely
extended at the end of his right. "May we
never want a friend in need, or a bottle to give
him ! Overhaul the Proverbs of Solomon, and
when found make a note of," we hear him
saying ; and then we follow him through those
inimitable scenes which cannot be easily for-

gotten **by those who** witnessed them. **The**
scene where he cheers up *Florence*, and makes
such dexterous play with his hook, adjusting
her bonnet and manipulating the tea—and yet
exhibiting a simple and **natural** pathos with **it
all**; where he sits in admiring contemplation
of *Bunsby*, while that oracular tar delivers his
celebrated **opinion** respecting the fate **of the**
vessel, **with the** memorable addendum: " The
bearings of this observation lays in the appli-
cation on it "; the scene with the *MacStingers*,
and the *Captain's* despair; **the** timely inter-
vention of *Bunsby;* **the** despair changed to
wondering awe; and then all the suggestive
by-play consequent upon his delivery by
Bunsby from the impending *MacStinger* ven-
geance;—all this, **and** much more than we can
describe, passes by like a panorama in memory.
Burton's *Captain Cuttle* occupies a conspicuous
place **in the** gallery of famous dramatic pictures, and there it will long remain.' **As we**

¹ Ireland, in referring to certain qualities of Burton's acting, **says**: " While in homely pathos, and the earnest expres-

think of it in all the details which made it so
perfect an embodiment, it seems a pity that
Dickens himself never saw it. We can fancy
that had he chanced to be in New York when
" Dombey and Son " was the theatrical sensation, and had dropped in at Chambers Street,
an auditor all unknown, he would have made
his way behind the scenes, and to Burton's
dressing-room, and with both hands would
have grasped the comedian's hook and enthusi-
astically shaken it.

" The Serious Family " and " The Toodles "!
What memories of joyous, laughing hours the
names awaken! Never, we venture to say,
were playhouse audiences regaled with so
surpassing a feast of mirth as that spread by
Burton in his performance of those renowned
specialities—*Aminadab Sleek* and *Timothy Toodles.* No comedian, we believe, of whom we

sion of blunt, uncultivated feeling, he has rarely been excelled.
His grief at the supposed death of Walter Gay, or poor Wally,
as Captain Cuttle affectionately called him, was one of the
most touching bits of acting ever witnessed, and has wrung
tears from many an unwilling eye."   .

have any record, excelled those efforts in
variety of mimetic effect, facial expression,
and display of comic power. That in them
the extreme limit of humorous demonstration
was reached, the public generally acknowl-
edged. The two plays had their regular
nights, and thousands flocked, week after
week, to the banquet of jollity, all unsatisfied,
though again and again they had revelled
there. No greater contrast could be offered
an audience than that presented by the two
pieces of acting. The sanctimonious and
lugubrious *Sleek;* the effusive and rubicund
Toodles! Coming one after the other, in every
way so different, the instance of versatility
made a deep impression, and prompted a
thought on the flexibility of human genius.
We are reminded at this moment of an incident which occurred one evening in connection
with " The Serious Family," which added an
unexpected feature to the entertainment.
Burton did not appear in the first piece, and
the audience, eager for *Aminadab*, were glad

when the orchestra ceased. But the prompter's
bell did not tinkle. After a pause the orchestra played again, and again finished. Still no
bell. Signs of impatience began, and as the
delay continued the hubbub increased. An
attempt on the part of the musicians to fill
the gap was received with evident displeasure.
At last, when nearly half an hour had elapsed,
the bell sounded, and the curtain rose on the
familiar group of *Sleek*, *Lady Creamly*, and
Mrs. Torrens. Applause broke out all over
the house; but with it were mingled a few
ill-humored hisses. Burton left his place at
the table and came forward to the foot-lights.
There he stood in the well-known suit of
pepper and salt, the straight gray hair framing
the solemn visage of *Sleek*. Then, in his own
proper voice, he explained the cause of the
delay—a mishap of travel,—expressed his
regret, and begged the indulgence of the
audience. A storm of approval followed his
speech, in the midst of which he resumed his
place, instantly assuming his character; and

MR. BURTON AS AMINADAB SLEEK

as the applause died away another voice succeeded, the voice of *Sleek*, in nasal tone, saying : " We appeal to the disciples of true
benevolence, and the doers of good deeds,
without distinction of politics or party," etc.
The effect of the transition was irresistible ;
and the loss of time was forgotten in the gain
of a new delight. And now another story of
" The Serious Family " comes to mind, and it
is too good to be lost. Playing in Atlanta,
Georgia, he found a wretched theatre, without
appointments or properties. At the conclusion of the overture the prompter ran to
Burton with the announcement that there
was no bell to ring up the curtain. " Good
gracious, what a place ! Here, my lad," he
said to a little fellow who acted as call-boy,
" run out and get us a bell—any thing will do
—a cow bell, if you can't get any thing better."
Away went the boy, the orchestra vainly en-
deavoring to quiet the audience with popular
airs. Back came the boy, pale and breathless,
gasping out : " There ain't a bell in the whole
town, sir ! "

"**What** 's to be done now?" asked the prompter.

"Shake the thunder!" No sooner said than done. Up went the curtain, and "The Serious Family" commenced amidst the most terrific peal heard in that theatre for many a year.

It goes without saying that Burton's *Sleek* **and** *Toodles*, especially **the** latter, though founded on another's outlines, were so built upon and humorously amplified, that in diverting **dramatic** effect they were clearly his own creations, and owed their importance to the **impress** of the actor's transforming power. When we read "The Serious Family" as written **ten by** Morris Barnett, clever though it be, we see at once where the author ends and **the** actor begins; and as for "The Toodles," it is sufficient to say that the *Timothy Toodles* of Burton was never dreamed of **by the** playwright.

How shall we describe to those who were born **too** late to witness them, these famous **performances of** the great comedian? We feel

that all description must fail in giving any idea
of the infinite variety and scope of comic
humor they exhibited. We might, indeed, for
they are vivid in remembrance, take our readers through the many scenes, and show them
Sleek, from the entrance of *Captain Maguire*, in
the first act, to Burton's enraged exit in the
last ; picturing, as we go, the situations without
parallel in droll device and mirth-moving complication ; show them *Toodles*, from his arraign-
ment of *Mrs. Toodles* for her multifarious and
preposterous bargains, not forgetting the *door-
plate* of *Thompson—Thompson* with a *p*—nor
"he had a brother,"—to his inimitable tipsy
scene and the memorable soliloquy, "That
man reminds me " ;—but, however exhaustive
the relation in words, after all was said, we
should still hopelessly leave the effect to be
guessed at with the help of imagination.

We have thus endeavored to give impressions from memory of certain parts in which
Burton was specially famous; and they seem
to us, on account of their versatility and range

of humorous spirit, to be conspicuous examples of that varied power which led us to style the comedian an expounder of the Humor of the Drama in all its aspects. If the sojourn on earth of old Robert Burton was intended to give the world an "Anatomy of Melancholy," surely the mission of the later Burton was to lay bare the whole body of mirth.

MR. BURTON IN COMEDY AND SHAKESPEARE.

As we think of the many parts in which it was our good fortune to see Mr. Burton, we are led into a reflection on the surprising versatility displayed by them; and we question whether the record of any comedian embraces a repertory so extensive, so varied, and so distinguished for general ability. The performances we are about to recall, though exhibiting many humorous features in common, were each a distinct conception; and the execution of each was a dramatic portrait by itself, artistic in measure, faithful in delineation, and felicitous in the expression of points of character.

The Burtonian element—in the shape of by-play, gesture, accent, facial **device,** mimetic effect—was visible in the composition, as a matter of course, contributing to the picture's expansion, deepening its tints and emphasizing its characteristics,—added touches that were the actor's stamp and sign-manual. We have cited *Sleek* and *Toodles* as strongly contrasting parts, and so indeed they were ; but we might easily adduce instances of versatility quite as **striking,** and would **do** so were it **not more** than likely that they will appear to our readers as our memories progress. It is said that the celebrated William Farren used to style him-self a " cock salmon," the only fish of his kind in the market; and if unique dramatic distinc-tion lies **in** that piscatorial image, most as-suredly Mr. Burton was a cock salmon of the first water.

We cannot hope to remember every thing we saw Mr. Burton play, yet we think our recollection will embrace a fair array of those characters in comedy and divers pieces which

he alone in his generation seemed adequately
to fill, and which were such a boon of delight
to the audiences of long ago.

There was his *Micawber*, in the dramatization of " David Copperfield," which succeeded
" Dombey and Son,"—equal to if not surpassing his *Cuttle ;* an inimitable reproduction
of the novelist's creation, full of humorous
point, and sustained with an indescribable airy
complacence and bland assumption of resource,
that made it a perfect treat to lovers of Dickens ; and those who saw " David Copperfield "
may well rejoice, for they hold in memory
Burton's *Micawber*, Johnston's *Uriah Heep*,
and Mrs. Hughes' *Betsy Trotwood !*

There was *Bumble*, the beadle, in "Oliver
Twist," a very funny piece of acting, and
especially so in the well-known scene with *Mrs.
Corney*, where, in excess of tenderness, he tells
her that "any cat, or kitten, that could live
with you ma'am, and *not* be fond of its home,
must be a ass ma'am." And then when the
matron is called away and the beadle remains,

his proceedings are described by Dickens thus: " Mr. Bumble's conduct on being left to him- self was rather inexplicable. He opened the **closet,** counted the teaspoons, weighed the sugar-tongs, closely inspected the silver milk- pot to ascertain **that** it was of the genuine metal, and, having satisfied his curiosity **on** these points, put on his·cocked hat cornerwise, and danced with much gravity four distinct times round the table. Having **gone through** this very extraordinary performance, he took off the cocked hat again, and spreading him- self before the fire with his back toward it, seemed to be mentally engaged **in** taking an exact inventory of the furniture." We deem it enough to say that Mr. Burton's management of the foregoing " business " left nothing to be desired.

We may note, in the mention of " Oliver **Twist,**" that *Nancy Sykes* was played by the late Fanny Wallack, with a fidelity of purpose and a pathetic abandon that made it painful to witness.

To continue with Dickens: there were *Squeers* and *Sam Weller*, both capital in their way—the last, however, lacking, as it seemed to us, in true Wellerian flavor; but the *Squeers* was marked by an appreciative recognition of . the schoolmaster's grim traits; and the scene at *Dotheboys Hall* was admirably given; Mrs. Hughes, as *Mrs. Squeers*, "made up" to the life, and irresistible in her distribution of the treacle.

All these portraits from the pages of Dickens were so many meritorious presentments of the novelist's creations, and would have won endur- ing fame for an actor of smaller calibre; the truth is, in Mr. Burton's case, that his *Bumble*, *Squeers*, and *Weller* were but dimly seen, owing to the greater glory of his *Cuttle* and *Mi- cawber*.

We saw Mr. Burton as *Bob Acres*, in "The Rivals"; as *Tony Lumpkin*, in "She Stoops to Conquer"; as *Goldfinch*, in "The Road to Ruin"; as *Doctor Ollapod*, in "The Poor Gentleman"; as *Sir George Thunder*, in "Wild

Oats."; as *Job Thornberry,* in " John Bull "; as
Sir Oliver Surface, in "The School for Scandal "; as *Graves,* in Bulwer's " Money "; as
the *Mock Duke,* in "The Honeymoon"; as
Adam Brock, in "Charles XII.''; as *Van
Dunder,* in " The Dutch Governor"; as *John
Smith,* in " Nature's Nobleman "; as *Mr. Sudden,* in " The Breach of Promise "; as *Thomas
Trot,* in " Paris and London "; as *Don Ferolo
Whiskerandos,* in " The Critic " of Sheridan ;
as *Triplet,* in " Masks and Faces ";—certainly a
gallery of dramatic portraits that would put
to the test the highest order of ability; and
we feel bound to say that Burton passed the
ordeal well deserving the encomiums that were
bestowed upon his efforts. It would be too
much **to** expect that all these delineations were
even **in** points of conception and execution ;
yet all were entitled to respectful consideration, and many **were** masterpieces. We will
endeavor to go through them briefly, in remembrance of the happy hours we owe to their joy-
ous influence.

The recent appearance of Jefferson as *Bob Acres* has aroused a new interest in the character, and from all accounts the performance was more than equal to expectation, and has enhanced the reputation of the comedian. **We** hope to have the pleasure of seeing **Mr.** Jefferson in due time, and we fancy that his acting **of *Acres*** would refresh somewhat our recollection of Burton in the part. As it is, however, we cannot.vouch for a clear memory of Burton's *Acres.* We saw it but once, and then early in life, when we were new to the theatre; and all **we seem to remember is that** he was very funny with his curl **papers, and** his "referential **or** allegorical swearing," and that the duel scene was very amusing. It was the opinion of **Hazlitt** that Sheridan overdid the part, and accordingly he goes on to say: "It calls for a greater effort of animal spirits and a peculiar **aptitude of** genius in the actor to go through **with it, to** humor the extravagance, and to seem to **take a** real and cordial delight in caricaturing himself." This criticism is not without force; but whatever may have been Burton's conception, **we are** certain that **a** bright intelligence informed it, and that in the portrayal a requisite display of " animal spirits " was not lacking.   If, among the audience that greeted Jefferson, there chanced to be any old play-goers of tenacious memory who had seen Burton, **let** us hope that they improved the occasion by pleasant reminiscence.

Tony Lumpkin was **a very** comic piece of acting, **and** made **the people** laugh immoderately; but we confess that the character has little charm **for us.**   Burton used **to** sing the song **of** " The Three Jolly Pigeons " **(in** the ale-house scene) with more expression than melody; but he threw into it a great deal of frolic spirit and made it quite a feature.

In our youthful days, when witnessing " The Road to Ruin," **we** knew very well the moment when we should **hear** the voice of *Goldfinch* outside; and we remember his bustling entrance, **in** sporting frock, buff waiscoat, and top boots, whip **in** hand, and his rattling flow of horse-talk; his strut and his "that 's your sort!" **It is** said that Lewis, of Covent Garden, (the original *Goldfinch*,) "gave to that catch-phrase a variety of intonation which made **it always new** and effective"; and Burton certainly played upon it adroitly. His delivery of the text was full **of** point and animation, and his articulation admirable. "Why, you **are a** high fellow, Charles," says *Harry Dornton*. "To be sure!" replies *Goldfinch*, "know **the odds—hold** four-in-hand—turn a corner in style—reins in form—elbows square—wrist pliant—hayait!—drive the Coventry stage twice a week all summer—pay for an inside place— **mount the box—tip** the coachy a crown—beat **the** mail—come in full speed—rattle down the **gateway—take care of** your heads!—never killed but one woman and a child in all my life—that 's your sort!" We hear Burton's **voice,** we see his face and his gestures now!

We were always fond of Colman's "Poor **Gentleman," and we** took great delight in **seeing Burton** as *Doctor Ollapod*. As all know, the character affords wide scope for diverting treatment. The incidents are many and **droll** —and we think Burton turned every thing to the best account. Henry Placide played the part more artistically ; but it was not possible for him **to expound its** humorous nature **with** the richness **that came easily** to Burton. We never think **of Colman's** comedy without a feeling of grateful pleasure ; for its representa- **tion at various times** gave **us** Burton and **Placide as** *Ollapod ;* **Burton as** *Sir Robert Bramble ;* Dyott, as *Worthington ;* Mrs. Hughes as *Lucretia McTab ;* **and** Johnston as *Humph- rey Dobbins.*

We have referred **in** another place to *Sir George Thunder* and *Job Thornberry ;* and we need not dwell upon them further than to say that both gave glimpses of that versatile power **to** which we have alluded, and both were full of the comedian's characteristic ability.

We suppose that *Sir Oliver Surface* **would** not be deemed **a** part exactly **in Mr.** Burton's "line"; **and** yet, as we remember it, he in-

vested the character with a simple dignity, and
played it with manly directness and feeling.

Our memory of *Mr. Graves* and the *Mock
Duke* is dim and distant; but if our readers
desire another example of versatility, we
commend the two parts as furnishing a most
conspicuous instance.

We have never seen "Charles XII." and
"The Dutch Governor" since we saw Burton
as *Adam Brock* and *Van Dunder;* but we
assure the play-goers of to-day that the dramas
were well worth seeing long ago when Liston
played in them, and equally so when his great
successor appeared in them at a later period.
Burton rarely played *Adam Brock*, and we
cannot remember seeing it more than once,
when it impressed us greatly. "The Dutch
Governor," on the contrary, was a favorite
attraction at the Chambers Street Theatre,
and Burton's *Van Dunder* was a rich feast of
mirthful enjoyment.

Pardey's "Nature's Nobleman," purporting
to be an American comedy, was first produced

at **Burton's** in **1851.** The prologue, which was
spoken by the manager, contained **these lines:**

> " The drama languishes. Let **us** detect—
> Polonius-like—the cause of this defect !
> **'T is certain that** the sprightliest tongue must fail
> To win attention **to an** ' oft-told tale.'
> We cannot, **ever, with** ' crook'd **Richard** ' fight,
> Or weep with Desdemona every night ;
> And even cloying is the luscious sack,
> If we too often sip with ' burly Jack ' ;
> Nor, **every** week, will people take the trouble
> To witness Hecate's cauldron hiss and bubble **;**
> Nor can we, **as we** have done, hope to draw
> Still on the Rivals or the Heir-at-Law.
> We 've seen shy ' Jack ' his father's anger **rouse ;**
> We 've heard Lord Dowlas ' tutored ' by his spouse.
> Old English comedy should now give **way ;**
> It has, like Acres' ' dammes,' had its day.
> Hang up bag wigs—our study now should be
> The men and the moustachios that we see.
> Let **us** some pictures of the time provide **;**
> Let the pen practically be applied."

Whether or no the comedy gave us " the
men and the moustachios **that** we see," or pro-
vided **" some pictures** of the time," we shall
not pretend to say ;—one would think so, since
Blake, Burton, **Bland,** Dyott, Mrs. Hughes,
Mary Taylor, Miss Weston, and Caroline Chap-

man were in the cast,—but, at all events, it
gave us Burton's *John Smith*, which was well
worth a journey to see. *John Smith* is " gentleman " to the *Earl of Leamington* (Dyott), who
is making an American tour. The *Earl* gives
his attendant a two-months' holiday to enjoy
himself ; and *Smith*, having dressed within an
inch of his life, is taken for the *Earl*, and yields
to the temptation to **pass** himself off as such.
Out of this complication arise situations ludicrous in the extreme, through which Burton
moved, the dispenser of mirth without end.
His " make-up," his air, his self-sufficiency, his
ignorance,—of which he is grotesquely uncon-
scious,—**his** blundering malapropos speeches,
his frequent social collapses and absurd at-
tempts at recovery, his facial expression at
mental mishap and irresistible by-play conse-
quent, his constant display of mimetic power,
his voice, look, manner,—all together made a
picture of varied humor, which kept the house
in hearty laughter from his entrance to the
curtain's fall.

Mr. Sudden, in Buckstone's "Breach of Promise," was still another of those peculiar parts upon which Burton lavished his supreme gift of humor; and we owe to its diverting exposition many a gladsome hour.

Funny, too, beyond measure, were *Thomas Trot* and *Don Whiskerandos;* we see the first in the many comic incidents during the voyage from Paris to London; and we see *Don Whiskerandos* "quit this bustling scene" by rolling himself with marvellous celerity out of sight in the folds of the stage carpet.

We have reached the end of our string, with the exception of *Triplet*, and should love to linger in description on the blended humor and pathos of the impersonation. Let it suffice that not even Mr. Fisher's admirable presentment can dim the recollection of Burton's masterly delineation.

And now let us in our remaining space recall our memories of the Shakespearian parts in which we saw the great actor.

"A Midsummer-Night's Dream" was pro-

duced at Burton's in 1854, and the manager
played *Bottom.* We well remember with what
delight the play was received, and what a
marked sensation was created by the scenery
and stage effect. The public wondered how so
much could be presented on so small a stage,
and its accomplishment was a theme of general
admiration. The fairy element was made a
beautiful **feature,** and the spirit of poetry
brooded over the whole production. The
unanimity of the press in its encomiums on the
revival was remarkable ; and no more emphatic
recognition of Burton's appreciation and knowledge of Shakespeare could be given than was
expressed in that approving accord.

As we think of it now, it seems to us that
Burton's idea of *Bottom* was the true one, and
we enjoyed the performance immensely. It is
very easy to make the character a sort of buf-
foon ; but nothing, of course, was further than
that notion from Burton's conception. Mr.
Richard Grant White gives, in his "Shakespeare's Scholar," an admirable analysis of

Bottom's characteristics, and at the **close**
remarks: "**As Mr.** Burton renders the char-
acter, its traits are brought out with a
delicate and masterly hand; its humor is ex-
quisite." We remember his acting in the scene
where the artisans meet for the distribution of
parts in the play to be given before the *Duke;*
—how striking it was in sustained individuality,
and how finely exemplified was the potential
vanity of **Bottom.** With what ingrained assur-
ance he exclaimed: " Let me play the lion too;
I will roar, that it will do any man's heart good
to hear me; I will roar, that I will make the
duke say, *Let **him roar** again, **let** him roar
again!*" He was capital, too, in the scene of
the rehearsal, and **in** his translation; and the
love scene with *Titania* aroused lively interest.
What pleased us greatly was the vein of engaging raillery which ran through his delivery of
the speeches to the fairies, *Cobweb, Peas-blossom,*
and *Mustard-seed.* It goes without saying, that
as *Pyramus* in the tragedy Burton created
unbounded amusement, and discharged the

arduous **part of the** ill-starred lover with entire
satisfaction to everybody.

Sir Toby Belch, in " Twelfth Night," was one
of Burton's richest performances, and we remember it with the greatest pleasure. It was
characterized by true Shakespearian spirit, and
was acted with an animation and unctuous
humor quite impossible to describe. The scene
of the carousal wherein *Sir Toby* and *Aguecheek*
are discovered ; the arrival of the Clown with
his " How, now, my hearts? Did you never
see the picture of we three?" and *Belch's*
greeting of "Welcome, ass,"—inaugurated an
episode of extraordinary mirth, in which **Burton** moved the absolute monarch of merriment.
The duel scene and the scene in the garden,
when *Malvolio* reads the letter, were full of the
comedian's diverting power ; and we can recall
no single instance of humorous execution
which more perfectly fulfilled all conditions.

Burton played *Touchstone* and *Dogberry*, as
has been mentioned ; but it was never our
good fortune to see him in either. We saw

him as *Caliban*, in "The Tempest"; as *Autolycus*, in "Winter's Tale"; and as *Falstaff*, in
"The Merry Wives of Windsor." His *Caliban*
we have tried to forget rather than remember;
it terrified us and made us dream bad dreams;
but for all that, we know that it was a surprising impersonation. His *Autolycus* was a model
of oily roguery, and another instance of that
wondrous versatility of genius with which the
comedian was endowed. Very dim in memory
is Burton's *Sir John Falstaff*. We remember
the scene in the Garter Inn, and the letters to
the merry wives, and, of course, the *dénouement*
of the clothes-basket, and the frolic at Herne's
Oak,—but we cannot go into detail; and we
always thought we should like Burton so much
better in the *Falstaff* of "Henry IV." The
mention of "Henry IV." reminds us that it
was once produced at the Chambers Street
Theatre, when Hackett played *Sir John* to
Lester Wallack's *Prince Hal;* and in order that
nothing might be lacking in honor to Shakespeare, Burton and Blake played the two *Car-*

riers in Scene I. of Act II. Fancy those two comedians with about twenty-five lines only between them in a play of five acts! But they must have covered themselves with glory.

We have endeavored in this retrospect to furnish a view of the comedian in a number **of** characters; and we think, however meagre our account, it still forcibly indicates the scope and range of Burton's abilities, and exhibits him in a wide scene of varied and striking dramatic **power.** We have depicted him in farce, in comedy, and in Shakespearian delineations; and it is not too much to say that generations will likely pass **ere his** fellow shall appear. We **have heard and read of** attempts being made by ambitious actors to revive his masterpieces, **and that** the efforts were highly commendable. Perhaps they **were—**

> " A substitute shines brightly as a king
>   **Until** a king be by."

www.ingramcontent.com/pod-product-compliance
Lightning Source LLC
Chambersburg PA
CBHW032010060726
47497CB00017B/2454